Campaign for Her Heart

Decades: A Journey of African American Romance, Book 12

By Patricia Sargeant

Campaign for Her Heart

Decades: A Journey of African American Romance, Book 12

By Patricia Sargeant

Published by Mediopolis Communications, LLC

Cover design: Ennel John Espanola

Interior layout: Formatting Fairies

ISBN-10: 0-9985366-3-6

ISBN-13: 978-0-9985366-3-7

All characters in this book are fiction and figments of the author's imagination.

www.PatriciaSargeant.com

Campaign for Her Heart

"Tell me what you've been doing the past thirty-one years?" Gwen's hunger pangs receded as she ate her garden side salad.

"Shouldn't we be talking about you?" Noah glanced up from his salad bowl. He'd flavored his vegetables with blue cheese dressing.

"I want to know about the person who would be my manager if I decide to campaign – and that's a huge 'if.'" Gwen sipped her tart lemonade as she studied Noah. She sensed him gathering his thoughts in the silence. Why was he reluctant to talk about himself?

"Since we last saw each other, I've worked on dozens of campaigns, mainly for local and state candidates."

"Your more recent clients have been influential incumbents and promising up-and-comers."

"Have you been following my career?" Noah's teasing smile looked forced.

"Don't flatter yourself." Gwen tried a quelling glance. It didn't seem to work. "I did an internet search on you a couple of days ago."

"Pity." Noah nudged aside his now empty salad bowl. "I thought you might still have a soft spot for me."

Gwen's heart fluttered like it so often had when she and Noah had dated. The fact that she might still have a soft spot for him was worrisome. "Are you flirting with me, Noah?"

"Would that be a bad thing?"

"Let me count the ways." Gwen set her empty bowl beside his. Her gaze took in the establishment's shabby chic décor, dark wood paneling and deep red accents. "If I decide to run for office, we'd have to keep our relationship professional."

"Of course." But his eyes reminded her that they weren't working together yet.

DEDICATION

To My Dream Team:

- *My sister, Bernadette, for giving me the dream;*
- *My husband, Michael, for supporting the dream;*
- *My brother Richard for believing in the dream;*
- *My brother Gideon for encouraging the dream;*

And to Mom and Dad always with love.

ACKNOWLEDGEMENTS

Thank you to Wayne Adrian Jordan for inviting me to be a part of this historic project. My thanks also to Edwina P. and Cynthia T. for providing feedback on the story's initial draft. Your support and encouragement are always deeply appreciated.

Note: Campaign for Her Heart is the 12th book in the Decades: *A Journey of African American Romance* series. This series was envisioned by author Wayne Adrian Jordan. It consists of 12 books, each set in one of 12 decades between 1900 and 2010. Each story focuses on the romance between African American protagonists as it also embraces the African American experience within that decade. The *Decades* authors hope readers find the stories informative as well as entertaining.

CHAPTER 1

"How could this be a coincidence?" The words were clipped with almost surgical precision. They brought Noah Barrow to an abrupt stop in the reception area of State Senator Dexter Jackson's office suite late Tuesday morning.

That voice...

He turned toward the front desk where two women and a man stood with their backs to him as they confronted the senator's hapless receptionist. That voice... It transported him thirty-one years into his past.

Noah ignored the man, and the woman who stood in the middle. He focused on the trio's spokesperson, the slender woman in the blue wool dress who stood directly in front of the receptionist. There was something so familiar about her. Her confident bearing. Her dancer's posture. The frost in her sultry voice could give the listener hypothermia.

"Perhaps I can help you." Noah hadn't made a conscious decision to test his mortality with the irritated constituents. The words had just come out. He glanced at the man and woman before returning his gaze to their spokesperson.

The space-time continuum rocked as he confronted familiar wide cocoa eyes. Noah's thoughts stuttered as his mind struggled to process coming face-to-face with the woman who'd broken his heart more than thirty years earlier.

"Gwen Taylor." He spoke her name like an incantation and waited for her to disappear. She didn't.

"Noah Barrow. What are you doing here?" Shock edged out the glow of frustration in her catlike eyes. Her dark winged eyebrows soared toward her hairline. The sharp cheekbones of her diamond-shaped face showed a hint of pink. Her full, bow-shaped lips parted in surprise.

"I'm Senator Jackson's campaign manager."

"I see." Gwen packed several messages into those two words, including her opinion that he hadn't changed in three decades. At least she'd found a new target for her irritation.

Gwen's gaze cooled as she took in his cream shirt, navy tie and dark blue pants. He'd left his matching jacket in the small conference room that served as his office Tuesdays, Wednesdays and Thursdays. The rest of the week – and most weekends – Noah worked from his own office suite where he ran his political consulting firm. He wished he was there now. He and Gwen hadn't parted on the best of terms. The look in her eyes told him she hadn't forgotten, either.

Noah's gaze slid from Gwen's modest pearl stud earrings to her dark blue wool winter coat, which she'd hooked over her left arm. The garment looked warm enough to beat back the brisk late-February weather. Noah noticed her bronze Timex wristwatch – but no wedding ring.

Gwen gestured toward the couple with her. The man and woman appeared close in age to Gwen. "Kenneth and Cynthia Anthony. Noah Barrow."

"We've heard of you," Kenneth said as the couple exchanged handshakes with Noah.

Noah released Cynthia's hand. "You were asking for Senator Jackson. Can *I* help you?"

"We've had an eleven-thirty meeting on the books with Dexter for two weeks." Cynthia's wide brown eyes sparkled with curiosity as she looked from Gwen to Noah. "Where is he?"

Noah was almost a foot taller than Cynthia, but she still managed to look down her nose at him. Her expression enhanced her air of royalty. She'd gathered her thin honey brown braids into a bun that crowned her head. Chunky gold jewelry, a flowing gold sweater and matching wide-legged woolen pants added to her regal image.

"Let's talk in my office." He gestured down the hallway. "We'll be more comfortable."

Cynthia arched an eyebrow. "You mean *you'll* be more comfortable."

Noah wouldn't bet money on that. The trio's collective irritation with Dexter was like radioactive fallout. At least by moving their discussion to his private office, Noah could minimize the public hazard. At best, by meeting with them, he could diffuse the situation in a manner that would – hopefully – protect his client's image for reelection.

At the door to the small monochrome conference room, Noah stood back to allow Gwen, Cynthia and Kenneth to enter his temporary office. As Gwen walked past him, Noah fisted his hands. His twitchy fingers wanted to tunnel into her thick raven hair. When he'd known her in 1981, she'd worn a short pixie cut that had emphasized her features, especially her wide eyes and high cheekbones. Now her hair was longer and swept back from her forehead to frame her face.

Noah gestured for Dexter's guests to join him at the circular blond wood conference table. Gwen had the chair to his right.

Kenneth was on his left, a tall, broad imposing presence in a navy pinstriped suit and silver tie. His close-cropped hair had a light dusting of gray. Behind silver-rimmed eyeglasses, Kenneth's piercing almond-shaped black eyes probably deciphered other people's thoughts before they had them.

"This is the second time your boss has been 'unavoidably detained' from meeting with us." Gwen had repeated the phrase Noah had heard Dexter's receptionist use. "If we were showing up unannounced, that would be one thing, but our meetings have been scheduled in advance and confirmed more than once."

The statement stood in the space between them like scorched earth. Noah tried not to remember the effect Gwen's husky voice had had on him when she wasn't spitting angry.

He pulled his gaze from Gwen and sent it around the table. "I'm sure Senator Jackson's sorry about these scheduling conflicts. Unfortunately, we can't foresee them. Meetings sometimes run over."

He hoped his disarming smile masked the fact that he was lying through the teeth. Noah had access to the senator's calendar and had committed Dexter's schedule to memory. He knew this meeting with Gwen and her associates was the only event Dexter had scheduled for this morning. It was tagged as "Nuisance" and slotted for the hour between eleven-thirty and twelve-thirty. Dexter had left his office at eleven, and hadn't told anyone where he was going or when he'd be back.

Coincidence? Not likely.

He'd joined Dexter's campaign February first. Less than three weeks later, he was having second thoughts.

"We don't want Dexter's *apology*." Cynthia emphasized her last word with air quotes that she made with the index and second fingers of both of her hands. "We want him to work with us."

Kenneth rested his right forearm on the table's surface and shifted to better face Noah. "Jackson needs to do his job."

Noah kept his disarming smile in place. This wasn't his first rodeo. He'd handled angrier audiences than these three. "I can't interrupt Senator Jackson's meeting."

"No, that would be disrespectful." Gwen's cool tone stung like ice. "Not unlike the disrespect he continues to show us. The issues we're trying to bring to the senator's attention – police racial profiling, and stop-and-frisk, among others – are critical to ensuring the safety of our community."

Dexter had been wrong to pull his disappearing act, but Noah could understand why the senator had made himself scarce. This social justice group had come with an agenda – and questions his client wasn't equipped to answer. The realization added to Noah's doubts about working with Dexter.

"Senator Jackson takes these issues very seriously." The glints of anger in their eyes told Noah that Gwen, Cynthia and Kenneth had smelled the lie on his breath. "He wants to discuss them with you, but since he's not here, why don't you tell *me* your concerns and I'll have Senator Jackson email his response to you?"

"No." Kenneth appeared to be a man of few words, but he didn't need any others to convey his meaning. Dexter had lost Kenneth's vote.

Gwen raised her long, elegant fingers one at a time. "We've sent letters and emails. We've made phone calls and left messages. The last time he stood us up, we discussed our concerns with his receptionist. So tell us, Noah, how will discussing our concerns with *you* advance our cause?"

Cynthia crossed her arms. Her fingertips with their gold-polished nails drummed her elbows. "It won't."

Noah made one last effort to salvage the situation. "Then why don't we reschedule the meeting? Senator Jackson'll make time for you."

"*Make time* for us?" Cynthia lifted one perfectly arched dark eyebrow.

"We've heard that before." Kenneth's tone was thick with disgust.

"The senator should do more than hope that *we'll* make time for *him* on Election Day." Gwen's tone gave Noah frostbite and flashbacks to their breakup.

"Gwen, this time, you have my personal commitment." Noah held her scalding gaze. She was fire and ice.

Gwen angled her small, pointed chin. The gesture was disconcerting and disconcertingly familiar. "Senator Jackson has fooled himself into a false sense of security."

"Or maybe he's just a fool," Cynthia interrupted.

Gwen continued. "His reelection isn't guaranteed. The community that he's supposed to be serving is aware that he's been missing in action for quite some time. The fact is, Noah, your client is vulnerable in a primary."

"By whom?" Noah felt a stirring of alarm.

Gwen leaned into the table, closer to Noah. "The majority of people who put Dexter in office voted for the party's platform, *not* for Dexter. We're willing and able to find someone else, someone who'll actually work for us."

Noah considered the trio around the table. Were they bluffing? Could he risk it?

Noah sat back on his cushioned seat. "I hear your frustration and I understand. Senator Jackson *is* here to work for you and he has the support of the party to prove that."

Cynthia blew a scathing breath. "You are sadly mistaken if you think we need the party's support to run a candidate against Jackson."

Gwen nodded her agreement. "We the people elect our public servants, not the party. But then, the senator isn't in office to serve the people, is he? He's serving himself."

Noah lifted his hands, palms out. "Senator Jackson is concerned about the community that gave him the honor of representing them-"

"This meeting is over, Noah." Gwen stood, cutting of Noah's words. Cynthia and Kenneth rose with her.

Cynthia gathered her black clutch bag. "I've had as much bull manure as I can take."

Kenneth stood beside his wife. The look in his dark eyes said it all.

Noah rose, masking his dismay. "Gwen, let's reschedule."

Gwen stopped with her hand on the doorknob. "After all these years, you still don't understand. Politics isn't a game, Noah. It's a service. This isn't about one side winning and another side losing. It's a privilege to be chosen to protect a community. But when public servants don't serve the people, everybody loses."

Three votes walked out the door. How many more were they taking with them?

Noah rubbed the back of his neck. He had to fix this latest campaign problem. He had the experience, but did he have the will?

The better question was, did he have the right candidate?

***

"That smells delicious." Edwina Lemond stood in Gwen's office doorway early Tuesday afternoon. The technical services librarian wore a deep red cable knit sweater and tailored ebony slacks that looked both warm and comfortable.

"It tastes delicious, too, if I say so myself." Gwen set aside the homemade jerk chicken salad she was eating at her desk. The spicy chicken, crisp lettuce and sweet raisins made her taste buds sing.

Edwina settled onto one of the two powder blue cushioned visitor's chairs in front of Gwen's walnut wood desk. "How'd the meeting go with your least favorite state senator?"

Gwen had told Edwina about her plans to take an early lunch to meet with Dexter Jackson.

More than seven years ago, Gwen had hired Edwina to replace her as technical services librarian when Gwen had been promoted to director of the Metropolitan Public Library. They'd soon become good friends after realizing all they had in common, including a passion for serving their community.

Gwen spun her ancient blue padded executive chair to face the other woman. "Senator Jackson was once again missing in action. This time, he left his campaign manager, Noah Barrow, to cover for him."

Edwina's dark brown eyes stretched wide with a mixture of surprise and temper. "How much help was the campaign manager?"

"None at all. All he could do was lie for his boss. He knew that the senator was deliberately avoiding us. Again." Gwen rubbed her eyes.

She wanted to erase the images of Noah's rugged good looks. They'd brought back the sweet pain of those thirty-one-year-old memories. They'd been so young. He'd smelled great, too, just as he had when they'd been in love. She'd caught his scent as she'd walked past him into his office. Soap and mint. But those remembrances were distractions. She needed to remain focused.

"Jackson's afraid that if he supports our cause, he'll lose the police unions' endorsements." Edwina ran her long, slim fingers through the wavy dark brown hair that framed her heart-shaped face.

Gwen pressed her clasped hands against the hard, cool surface of her desk. "He doesn't have to take sides. He just needs to do what's right. Study after study has shown that black and brown people are over policed, over criminalized and over incarcerated. We must create policies that prevent these discriminatory practices."

"Especially when studies have also shown that domestic terror by nationalist militia groups is the real threat to national safety. The government is focusing on the wrong people."

They kept preaching to the choir. They were painfully aware of the statistics. How could they convince the government to act on them?

Gwen's gaze dipped to the salad waiting at the corner of her desk. Her appetite was gone. Even the raisins couldn't coax it back. "We need a new strategy for the senator."

"We need a new senator." Edwina scowled. "These incumbents get too comfortable in office. They forget what it means to be a public servant. They think they're supposed to 'govern' us when they're actually supposed to be serving our interests."

Gwen drummed her fingers on her desk. The sound faded into the background as she considered her options. "Term limits would help."

"That might get Jackson's attention. Senator *Jackson*. Humph! He's more like Senator *Jack-*"

"We've been too diplomatic, too status quo. Maybe he would be more responsive to threats."

"What kind of threats?" Edwina sounded intrigued.

"I told Noah that if the senator-"

"*Noah*? That sounds awfully cozy."

Gwen hoped she wasn't blushing under her friend's much too observant gaze. "The senator's campaign manager and I were... We dated for a while. It was more than thirty years ago."

Edwina's gaze sharpened. "Really? Small world."

Too small. "I warned Noah that if the senator continued to ignore the very real concerns in our community, we would run a candidate against him in the primary."

"Ooh. What did your Noah say to that?"

"First, he's not 'my Noah.' Second, I couldn't tell whether his concern was real."

"I like your idea, though. I like it a lot." Edwina gave Gwen an approving look. "If we can't get these deadbeat politicians out through term limits, then we need to challenge them at the polls."

Gwen blinked her surprise. "Edwina, it was an empty threat. The primary is June fifth. That's only fifteen weeks away. That's not enough time to find and prepare a candidate to oppose the senator."

"We don't have time to negotiate with an indifferent incumbent, either. Lives are at risk."

"Then we have to find a way to *make* him care." The clock in Gwen's mind ticked ever louder, moving inexorably toward June fifth.

"You have; we primary him." Edwina was firm. "Even if the challenger isn't chosen in the primary, the fact that we took a stand against Dexter will scare him enough to get his attention."

But would it keep his attention?

"At least it will further the conversation and give us a larger platform for the issues. All right, we'd better start the search. I'll talk with Cynthia and Kenneth. They have a lot of connections in the community. They'll be able to tell us if there's a capable candidate to primary the senator."

"I'll check with my contacts, too." Edwina unfolded herself from her seat. "Surely, someone can recommend a challenger for jack hole."

Gwen watched Edwina stride from her office. She wished she had Edwina's deep reserves of optimism.

At this late date, where would they find a candidate who's both credible to their community and knowledgeable about the issues that mattered to them?

***

Anger carried Noah into Dexter's office late Tuesday afternoon. He closed the door with a snick instead of a slam, a testament to his self-restraint. "Where were you?"

Dexter looked up from his cell phone text. "Who are you, my wife?"

It was three in the afternoon. Dexter had been gone since eleven o'clock in the morning. In light of that, Noah's question wasn't unreasonable. But Dexter appeared to find all questions directed toward him to be unreasonable.

The state senator's prickly nature conflicted with a key ingredient of his political success: approachability. To his constituents, Dexter was the friendly, next-door-neighbor. His youthful energy reinforced that false impression. His round, ageless face and clean-shaven head made him look younger than his sixty-plus years. People somehow overlooked his gold Rolex, dispassionate brown eyes and the expensive silk suits that were tailored to make his chubby figure look slimmer.

"You intentionally missed the meeting with the community activists." Noah made the observation a statement. What was the point in pretending he had any doubt?

Dexter's eyes glittered with mirth. "What did you tell 'em?"

"You can't put off your constituents, especially activists like Gwen Taylor and her friends."

"Three people." Dexter made a rude noise. "I'm not losing sleep over those votes."

"Those *three* people represent the majority of people in your district. They're bringing to you issues that matter to a large group of your voters."

That seemed to finally connect with Dexter. He lowered his cell phone and spun his new and expensive black leather executive chair to face Noah. "That Taylor woman probably has a lot of clout in her community."

"I'm sure she does." Noah felt a frisson of unease.

"Smear her."

Noah frowned. Had he heard Dexter correctly? "What?"

"Find dirt on Taylor and get it into the media." Dexter sent Noah an impatient glare before returning his attention to his cell phone. Clearly, the senator thought the conversation as over.

He was very much mistaken.

Noah's twinge of unease became a wave of anger. He struggled to keep his voice level. "I'm not running a negative campaign. You need to stay on message, once we find one. And meet with your constituents, starting with Gwen Taylor, and Kenneth and Cynthia Anthony."

"Are you being serious with me right now?" Dexter spread his hands, one of which still cupped his cell phone. "This is how you're going to campaign for me?"

"I'm not digging up dirt on anyone, especially not a private citizen whose only mistake is expecting you to do your job."

A spark of anger flashed in Dexter's dark brown eyes. "She's threatening my reelection." He pointed the index finger of the hand that held his cell phone toward Noah. "Get this straight: Anyone who isn't *with* me is against me. Understand?"

"I told you from the beginning that I don't work on negative campaigns."

Dexter gave Noah a dismissive look before returning to his texts. "You went negative for Cooper."

Noah stiffened at the reference to State Representative Thomas Cooper's campaign. It wasn't a shining moment. "That was almost twelve years ago, and it's one of the reasons I won't run a negative campaign ever again."

"Too bad." Dexter continued texting. "I'd rather work with *that* guy than the one you say you've become."

"Fine. I'll resign from your campaign." Noah turned toward the door.

"What? Wait. Where are you going? Can't you take a joke?"

Noah ignored Dexter's entreaties. Taking on Dexter as a client had been a mistake. He wasn't going back. He'd already invested twenty days into the state senator's campaign, and that had been twenty days too many.

Noah strode into his makeshift office. He turned off his laptop and shrugged into his navy blue suit jacket. Dexter had said all he needed to say and Noah had made his position clear. The tone of the senator's reelection campaign was Dexter's choice just as it was Noah's decision whether to manage the campaign. He wouldn't.

Noah packed his laptop and collected his overcoat. He didn't have any regrets over his decision to break ties with Dexter. That was a good sign. It meant he was making the right move.

What should his next right move be?

CHAPTER 2

The next morning, Dexter's name popped up on the caller identification display of Noah's business cell phone. The argument could be made that Noah should have expected Dexter's call. The state senator wasn't the kind of guy to fade quietly into the past.

Noah spun his padded, black cloth executive chair to face the panoramic view from the window behind his office desk. "Hello, Dexter."

"Where are you?"

Oh, the irony. Dexter's question was a variation of the one Noah had asked yesterday after Dexter had returned from his four-hour lunch. He was tempted to give Dexter back his response: Who are you, my wife?

With an effort, Noah rose above his baser instincts. "I resigned from your campaign, remember?"

From the window of his third-floor suite, Noah could see the office complex's parking lot. It was the last Wednesday of February. Mounds of snow surrounded the naked trees that framed the landscaping. It was cold outside with temperatures in the high twenties to low thirties, but the office suite was comfortable with just a bit of a chill to keep him and his five-member team awake.

"You were serious?" Dexter's raised voice expressed a complicated mixture of shock, irritation and confusion.

"Yes. I emailed my resignation last night. I'm sure you have it by now." Noah rose from his chair and stepped closer to his office window. He felt the February air leaking through the glass.

Dexter snorted. "We had one disagreement and you jumped ship? We have a contract."

"Which stipulates that I don't run negative campaigns." Behind him, Noah heard the sounds of his modest staff at work. The hum of conversations, clicking of computer keyboards, footsteps moving back and forth from the kitchenette/coffee station conveniently located across the hall from his office.

"One or two negative statements don't qualify as being a negative campaign." Dexter's tone was growing increasingly agitated.

Noah wasn't enjoying this conversation, either. Seeing himself as Dexter's campaign manager through Gwen's eyes had been a wake-up call. "You told me to launch a media attack against a private citizen, one of your own constituents. I don't work that way, not anymore."

Someone was brewing a fresh pot of coffee. Noah smelled it from across the hall. He hoped it wasn't Stuart. His firm's volunteer coordinator always skimped on the grounds, which made his coffee taste more like flavored hot water.

"This is politics, Noah." Dexter was trying to talk tough. "I'm in it to win it."

The sound of computer keys tapping on the other end of the line signaled that this critical conversation about the future of the state senator's campaign didn't have the candidate's undivided attention. How serious was Dexter about his reelection? Not serious enough. Noah recalled his meeting with Gwen, Cynthia and Kenneth, and shook his head.

"You want to win? Stick to the issues that matter to your voters." Noah returned to his chair.

"Are you going to help me or not?"

"Will you stay on message and not go negative for your campaign?"

An angry grunt muscled down the line from Dexter's end of the call. "At least give me a recommendation for your replacement."

Noah couldn't give Dexter a referral. Friends didn't do that to friends. "Members of the state political party can give you recommendations."

There was a faint clicking noise from the other end of the line as though Dexter was playing with his pen. "The last time I asked for recommendations, everyone agreed that you were the best. Every single one. They all said you know how to play the game. I guess they were wrong. You've lost your edge."

Coming from Dexter, Noah took that as a compliment. "The other party has a lot of strong candidates ready to challenge you in the general election, Dexter. You're going to have to run a disciplined campaign. You can't do that when you're hurling gossip and spreading lies."

A loud thump sounded on the other end of the line. Had Dexter hit his desk with his open palm? "Listen, I play offense. You got that? When someone hits me, I hit right back and twice as hard. Four times as hard. If you don't get that, I don't need you."

Dexter disconnected the call without allowing Noah to respond. That was another tactic in the political game that was played, the Verbal Diss-and-Dash. He used to do the same thing. He'd been part of the problem. Now he wanted to be part of the solution.

Where would he find a candidate who could help him get on the right team?

***

Noah stood from the restaurant's booth seating late Wednesday afternoon and embraced his youngest son, Clark. As he stepped back, he caught the look of unease beneath the recent college graduate's usually sunny expression. "Jim isn't coming, is he?"

Clark folded his long lean frame onto the padded bench-style seating on the other side of the table. Noah followed his son's lead and prepared for the disappointment.

"He can't make it today." Clark shifted his attention to his menu. "Maybe next time."

Clark was a good-looking kid. Well, at twenty-two, his son was a grown man, wasn't he? Time had flown since he'd taught his baby boy how to ride a bike. Now his son was his height – six-foot-three – and had his mother's big brown eyes.

Noah hoped his smile didn't look as strained as it felt. "That's what we thought last time. And the time before that."

Clark shifted on the bench. "I'm sorry, Dad. You know how stubborn he can be."

"I'm the one who's sorry. I can't blame him." In fact, if the situation were reversed, Noah would react just like James. He and his eldest child had a lot in common. "I'm also sorry for putting you in the middle. I won't do that anymore."

Clark's sunny disposition was restored. "That would be a relief."

The restaurant's server came to take their orders. The young man recorded Noah's request for ice water and Clark's preference for root beer before offering to take their meal choices. Clark ordered a Philly steak sandwich with fries. Noah bit back a groan of envy for the youth and fitness that allowed his son to eat whatever he wanted. Aware that at fifty-eight he had to be more restrained, Noah asked for a garden side salad and a turkey sandwich on whole grain, no mayo or cheese. Instead he splurged on mustard and jalapeno peppers.

Once their server left, Noah peppered Clark with questions about his week, his day and plans for his weekend. He was anxious to know everything that was happening with at least one of his children.

"I'm getting more confident with my projects." Clark paused as their young server brought their drinks.

Since graduation, Clark had been working in the Information Technology Services Department of one of the larger state universities. It was a job that helped pay his bills, but his ultimate goal – his dream – was to design computer games.

"I'm proud of you, son." Noah drank more water. He was still trying to ease the bitter disappointment of James's rejection. "Take advantage of the professional development opportunities your employer offers. You need to keep up with your industry's trends and advances."

Both of Noah's children were healthy and successful. Their mother, God rest her soul, would be proud. He was thankful that he'd never had to worry about James or Clark. Ever. He only wished they could say the same about him.

"I will." Clark nodded.

"Remember what Tupac said about the road being hard, but never giving up."

Clark flashed a grin. "Another Tupac quote."

Tupac Shakur, the West Coast rap artist and son of civil rights activist Black Panther Party member Afeni Shakur, was one of Noah's favorite rappers. He'd died too soon in 1996 at the age of twenty-five. Still in that short period of time, he'd had an enormous impact on music, fashion, culture and politics.

"He'll always be the best." Noah liked to think his sons got their love of rap music from him, but they were very much their own men.

"I don't know, Dad." Clark shrugged. "Nas has some mad skills."

Noah was familiar with the young New York rapper Nasir bin Olu Dara Jones, the eldest son of the jazz and blues musician Olu Dara. "Nas is a talented rapper in his own right, but Tupac will always be the best."

"All right, Dad. I know your loyalty to Tupac will never be swayed." Clark waited while the server delivered their entrees before continuing. "Now tell me what's bothering you."

Noah sprinkled ranch dressing over his salad as he gathered his thoughts. The scent of vegetable oil and salt from Clark's fries made his mouth water. "I've resigned from Dexter Jackson's reelection campaign."

Clark paused in the act of bathing his steak fries in ketchup. "What happened?"

Noah walked his fork through his salad, gathering bits of lettuce, carrots, cucumbers and tomatoes. "Dexter isn't running for reelection because he wants to serve the community. He's out to serve himself, and he plans to win by any means necessary."

"That didn't used to bother you. What's changed?" Clark bit into his Philly Cheesesteak sandwich.

Noah had a flashback to his first paid position on a political campaign and the memory of electric cocoa eyes that challenged him to find a greater meaning. Thirty-one years later, those same eyes had issued the same challenge yesterday. He could still smell

Gwen's lavender perfume. "I'm burned out on the system. Maybe I should leave politics altogether and just retire."

"I'm glad you left Senator Jackson's campaign." Clark shrugged. "You're right. He's a con."

Surprise made Noah temporarily speechless. "You were going to vote against my client?"

Clark tossed him another quick grin. "It wouldn't have been the first time. Mom voted against your clients sometimes, too."

Noah gaped at his son. "She told you that?"

"Yep, and asked me not to tell you." Clark paused, cocking his head pensively. "For some reason, I think she'd want you to know now."

Noah felt the grief that swept over Clark with memories of his late mother. That emotion was the reason he didn't ask any other questions. Noah finished his salad in silence, then turned to his turkey sandwich. "Part of me hopes someone primaries Dexter. He treats politics like a game."

Clark gave Noah a confused look. "You've been doing the same thing."

"I've been wrong." Noah felt tired to his bones.

"Look, Dad, you're really good at what you do. You shouldn't retire while you still feel passionate about your work." Clark gestured toward Noah with a steak fry. "Maybe it's not your career that's really bothering you. Maybe it's your clients. You just have to find better ones."

"And where would I find him-" Noah cut himself off as he caught another mental image of flashing cocoa eyes. "Or her?"

***

Noah rode the elevator to James's twelfth-floor apartment early Wednesday evening. He squared his shoulders, then pressed the doorbell. His gaze caught the peephole in the blonde wood door. Would his son answer – or pretend not to be in? Noah's lips curved wryly. He'd seen James's car in the underground parking garage.

Noah had raised his hand to press the bell a second time when the door was yanked open from the other side. "Is Clark all right?"

"Yes. He's probably home. I'm sure he's fine, son." Looking at James was like looking at himself in a mirror thirty years ago.

"Don't call me that." They were off to a less-than-promising start. "Why are you here?"

Sorrow pressed down on Noah. How had he allowed his relationship with his oldest child to degenerate so badly? "I came to see you. May I come in?"

James crossed his arms over his chest. "Whatever you have to say, say it here. And make it fast."

Noah wasn't surprised. He asked to be let in every time and every time the answer was the same. This treatment was no more than what he deserved. Noah recognized that, but it still hurt. "I want to apologize again. I don't know what else I can do or say to earn your forgiveness."

James's eyes were blocks of black ice. "Talk is cheap. Actions speak louder."

"I moved here to be closer to you."

"You came here when Clark decided to attend your alma mater."

"You've declined all of my invitations for us to spend time together, either alone or with Clark."

"I wish you'd had as much interest in spending time with us even twelve years ago."

The old words made fresh wounds. "I'm sorry, James. I know that I let you and Clark down when you needed me most. I'm trying to make amends."

"Make amends?" James dropped his arms. "You should have made amends thirteen years ago, right after Mom died."

Noah flinched. "I-"

"Mom died and you fell apart. Clark and I lost both of our parents in one night."

"You-"

"I was fourteen. Clark was nine. *You* were hurting, but *we* were hurting, too. You'd lost your *wife*. We lost our *mother*."

"It-"

"He was *nine*. I had to step up to help Clark deal with losing Mom, but there was no one to step up to help *me*." James beat his chest. "Clark was leaning on me. You were leaning on a bottle. What was *I* supposed to lean on?"

Noah heard thirteen years of anger, fear and confusion. Powerful emotions he had to break through to reach his son – if James would let him. "Son-"

"Don't call me that!" James's voice was tortured. "Do you remember *anything* from those years?"

"I remember fear." Noah cleared his throat. This wasn't the first time James had asked him that or the first time he'd answered. He'd keep answering this same question if it would give him back his son. "Clark's fear. Your fear. My fear."

"I had to call social services." James's voice cracked. His words were a plea – for understanding? For forgiveness?

"I put you in that position and I'm very sorry. You shouldn't blame yourself, son."

"Don't call me that!"

"Put the blame on me. Put it all on me. That's where it belongs."

"I don't blame myself. I know that it's your fault." But the look in James's eyes told Noah that they both knew he was lying.

"I've been sober for almost ten years."

James stared at him for long seconds in stony silence, then he stepped back and slammed the door in Noah's face.

Tears burnt Noah's eyes like acid. He wasn't hurting for himself. He was dying inside for his son who'd been forced to make a terrible decision in order to protect his younger brother. Noah wasn't the only one who was seeking forgiveness. Much of the anger James directed toward him was anger James felt for himself.

What could he do – what could he say – to convince his son to stop blaming himself?

CHAPTER 3

On the night of Sunday, February 26, 2012, in Sanford, Florida, George Zimmerman fatally shot Trayvon Martin, a seventeen-year-old African American high school student.

Gwen had woken to that news Monday morning. It had been three hours since she'd learned of it. Heard of it. Read of it. Now sitting at her desk in her office, she still couldn't process it. Not just because she lived in a predominately black community. Not just because she was the mother of black children. Not just because she had a black son.

She couldn't comprehend the level of hatred that would lead to the murder of a child who was walking home from a convenience store.

He was walking home from a convenience store.

Could someone - anyone - explain that to her?

Gwen's heart ached. Tears blurred her vision even as anger clenched her fists. She was having a fight-or-flight reaction to this latest injustice against her black and brown community. Her body was choosing to fight, but how could she when public servants such as Dexter Jackson wouldn't even engage?

Gwen slammed her coffee mug onto her desk. She tried again to concentrate on the draft of the mass email she planned to distribute to the library system's branches. She wanted to remind them of the bond issue on the upcoming June election ballot. It seemed insultingly trivial compared to the tragic news.

"I take it you've heard the reports about Trayvon Martin?" Edwina's voice, thick with emotion, came from Gwen's doorway. There were still a few minutes before the library opened.

Gwen took a long drink of her coffee to dislodge the bitter lump in her throat. Her steadying breath drew in the brew's rich scent. "So much for our post-racial society and the media's efforts to pat the United States on the back for electing a black president after only two-hundred-and-thirty-two years."

Edwina crossed into Gwen's office. Her ruby sweater enhanced the angry flush that highlighted her cheekbones. "Ah, yes, our post-racial society in which no one sees color anymore. That must be the reason so many jurisdictions support racial profiling."

Gwen recognized the important point wrapped in Edwina's dripping sarcasm. "Apparently hoodies are the modern-day equivalent of a bull's eye." She gave a watery sigh. "I can't even imagine the anguish that Trayvon Martin's parents are feeling over their son's senseless murder."

Edwina settled onto her usual chair on the other side of Gwen's desk. "The media's negative portrayal of black and brown people, and the justice system's unjust handling of black and brown communities gives the false impression that we're all up to no good. I have no doubt that's what was going on in that so-called neighborhood watch captain's mind when he saw young Trayvon. Standing his ground my-"

"I agree." Gwen turned her chair to face her friend. "They're not only killing us in the streets, they're committing psychological warfare on and about our communities."

"Sean Bell in the two-thousands. Amadou Diallo in the nineteen-nineties. And that's just the men."

Gwen gripped her cooling coffee mug between her palms. "When we protest these very real threats to our community, law enforcement agencies all the way up to the federal level criminalize and target our social justice activists."

"What are we going to do about it?"

"We need to elect public servants who understand the issues and the data – data which, by the way, proves we're not making this up. We need to elect people who will legislate our protection and enforce that legislation. Frankly, that's been the answer for the past two-hundred-plus years."

"Our community has been fighting these battles since long before either of us was born. The Negro Silent Protest Parade in 1917. The Selma to Montgomery marches in 1965." Edwina's sigh was weary. "How do we keep from giving up?"

How? Gwen's eyes again burned with tears of anger and regret. "My parents came here from the Dominican Republic in the nineteen-fifties. They were part of the nineteen-sixties' Civil Rights Movement. They often told me that when you know that the cause you're fighting for will improve the lives of millions of people for generations to come – black, brown, white, everyone – that goal and your hope will give you the strength and courage you need to continue the struggle."

"I know we need hundreds of public servants who actually serve." Edwina stood. The fire of determination burned in her dark eyes. "For now, I'd be happy to find just one."

"So would I." Gwen rubbed at the frown tightening her forehead. "The clock's ticking on this election cycle, and I don't even know where to look."

***

"I'm sorry to interrupt you, Gwen."

The high-pitched greeting interrupted Gwen's concentration Wednesday – Leap Day – as she reviewed the printout of the library system's end-of-month budget report. She pressed her pencil point against the top sheet to mark her place before she transferred her attention to Midge Pullen, her administrative assistant. It was a little after noon.

"You're fine. What is it?"

Midge lowered her voice and patted her graying red hair. Her powder blue eyes sparkled with curiosity. "Kenneth and Cynthia Anthony, and a very attractive, hopefully single man would like to speak with you."

Odd. Usually the couple called before they stopped by. And who was this friend? Gwen's stomach grumbled, prompting her to press her palm against it. She was hungry, but she could spare a few moments for library donors, especially when they were dear friends.

Gwen drew an asterisk to mark her place on the sheet of paper. "Thanks, Midge. Could you ask them to come in, please?"

"Sure, and could you get their friend's phone number, if not for you, then for me?" Midge disappeared down the hallway.

Moments later, Cynthia led her delegation into Gwen's office. "Sorry to come unannounced. You know that's not my way."

Gwen crossed her office to greet her guests. She struggled to keep her smile in place as her eyes met Noah's. He was the very-attractive-hopefully-single man Midge had mentioned. Why was Dexter's apologist in her office?

Both Kenneth and Noah wore conservative dark business suits and carried their winter coats. In contrast, Cynthia did her usual impression of a fashion-forward royal. She'd accessorized her flowing magenta pantsuit with matching stilettos and chunky amethyst jewelry. Kenneth helped her out of her sapphire winter coat.

"It's always nice to see you." Gwen embraced first Cynthia, then Kenneth before stepping back. "Noah. This is a surprise."

"From your tone, not a happy one." Noah offered his hand. His skin was warm and rough against Gwen's. As a campaign manager, he basically had a desk job, but based on the feel of his long fingers and wide palm, he still had interests that drew him outdoors.

Gwen released his hand, but her skin where he'd touched her was still warm. "That depends on whether you've brought us something more substantive than Senator Jackson's apologies or soon-to-be broken promises."

She gestured toward her small, circular conference table, which would comfortably fit four. Gwen hoped they hadn't heard her stomach grumble. She could almost taste the lentil soup with dumplings she'd packed for today's lunch.

"You're still brutally direct." Noah's deep, rumbling chuckle made Gwen think of sultry nights and eighties music.

Cynthia took the chair Kenneth held for her. "In fact, we've brought something much more meaningful than Dexter's words. We've chosen the perfect candidate to primary him on the June ballot."

Gwen slipped onto the closest chair, then watched as Kenneth and Noah took seats on either side of her. A surge of hope rushed through her, alleviating some of the weight that had grown even heavier since the news of Trayvon Martin's murder. "Who?"

"You." Cynthia's single syllable seemed to echo around the room in the silence that greeted her announcement.

Gwen couldn't have heard Cynthia correctly. Would her friend ask her to primary Dexter Jackson during a meeting with the incumbent senator's campaign manager? What was she missing? She turned to Kenneth, who was looking back at her. She glanced at Noah, who seemed amused.

"I'm sorry." Gwen returned her attention to Cynthia. "What is it that you want me to do?"

"Run against Jackson." Kenneth didn't make any more sense than his wife.

The look in Noah's midnight eyes told her he knew what she was thinking. He gave her his sexy half smile. "I'd like to manage your campaign."

The situation was getting stranger and stranger.

Noah emanated confidence and control. From their shared past, Gwen knew that he was an intimidating opponent. That's what made him a valuable ally. But where would his allegiance lay?

"That's a very generous offer, Noah." Gwen considered the politico. "How do you propose to manage my campaign and Senator Jackson's?"

"I've left the senator's campaign." Noah's eyes suddenly appeared shuttered. What was he hiding?

Gwen settled back on her chair. "What made you leave?"

"We had a difference of opinion." Noah's tone carried a subtle warning not to trespass.

Gwen ignored it. "What was it about?"

Noah must have seen the determination in Gwen's eyes. He gave an audible yet ineffective sigh. "Dexter wants to run a negative campaign. I don't manage negative campaigns. That's in my consultant contract."

Gwen's eyes widened. "Forgive me if I appear doubtful, but thirty years ago, you wouldn't have been opposed to negativity. You would have suggested it."

The younger Noah would have considered it all part of the game, like football players trash talking at the line of scrimmage or basketball players faking a fall to get to the free throw line. Maybe this mature Noah was more than a pretty face. Had he added principles to his arsenal of intellect, charm and confidence?

"Who did he want to smear?" Kenneth asked.

Noah met Gwen's eyes. "Gwen."

"Me?" Gwen was stunned.

"First he refuses to meet with us and now he wants to attack us?" Cynthia scowled. "Won't he be surprised when Gwen announces her candidacy?"

Gwen's stomach murmured again. Was hunger the reason for her confusion? Maybe she was hallucinating. "I'm flattered and honored that you think I'm qualified to represent our district in the state senate, but you know that I plan to retire in two years, three months, one week and one day."

"You're actually counting down the days?" Cynthia rolled her eyes.

Gwen spread her arms in a helpless gesture. "My plans for taking an early retirement don't include starting a new career. I just bought an armchair with a matching ottoman and a new bookcase."

Gwen envisioned her retirement so clearly. She'd dreamed of it, planned for it and anticipated it for so long. Instead of working long hours, weekdays, weekends and weeks, she'd curl up on her comfy armchair with the matching ottoman. Beside her would be her precious bookcase. She'd fill it with books that she would purchase from the book conferences she'd attend all over the country - maybe even the world. She'd take a break for lunch in the afternoon, stretch her legs in the evenings, then return to her armchair, matching ottoman and bookcase until late into the night.

Cynthia expelled a disgusted breath. "It was *your* idea to replace Dexter."

"I didn't mean with *me*." Gwen pressed her hand to her stomach again. The muted grumbling had become a low roar.

Cynthia continued without taking notice of Gwen's objection. "When Noah suggested we approach *you* about running against Dexter, we knew he was right."

Gwen turned her stunned eyes to Noah's. "*You* suggested that I run for office?"

Noah's gaze was steady. "If not you, then who?"

His question took her aback.

Cynthia swept her hand in a royal decree. "You'd be perfect."

Gwen shifted her stunned gaze from Noah's to Kenneth's, then Cynthia's. "Campaigning for public office isn't something that I'd *ever* imagined doing. Public service isn't something to take lightly."

"The fact you believe that is proof you're the person this community needs to represent us," Noah said.

Gwen tugged her left ear with its sterling silver stud earring. The idea of being in the statehouse to push forward legislation that would benefit her community had appeal. Boy, did it have appeal. But did she want to get into politics? She'd long considered it a cesspool of self-absorption and avarice, cowardly lies and self-serving deals. Did she want to join that club of corruption?

Gwen wanted to wring her hands. Instead she laid them flat on the smooth surface of the fake wood table. "This is a lot to think about."

Noah's dark eyes glinted with determination. "Why don't you and I discuss this further over lunch?"

Gwen pressed both hands over her applauding stomach. "Lunch would be nice."

***

The restaurant Noah drove them to was listed on Gwen's budget's No Try Zone, but since he was paying, she relaxed her restrictions.

"Tell me what you've been doing the past thirty-one years?" Gwen's hunger pangs receded as she ate her garden side salad. The balsamic vinaigrette dressing did a tangy tap dance on her taste buds.

She recognized several of the state's movers and shakers as she surreptitiously scanned the lunchtime crowd. Gwen wished she'd brought her proposal for a state police oversight commission. She'd hand deliver it to them during dessert.

"Shouldn't we be talking about you?" Noah glanced up from his salad bowl. He'd flavored his vegetables with blue cheese dressing.

"I want to know about the person who would be my manager if I decide to campaign – and that's a huge 'if.'" Gwen sipped her tart lemonade as she studied Noah. She sensed him gathering his thoughts in the silence. Why was he reluctant to talk about himself?

"Since we last saw each other, I've worked on dozens of campaigns, mainly for local and state candidates."

"Your more recent clients have been influential incumbents and promising up-and-comers."

"Have you been following my career?" Noah's teasing smile looked forced.

"Don't flatter yourself." Gwen tried a quelling glance. It didn't seem to work. "I did an internet search on you a couple of days ago."

"Pity." Noah nudged aside his now empty salad bowl. "I thought you might still have a soft spot for me."

Gwen's heart fluttered like it so often had when she and Noah had dated. The fact that she might still have a soft spot for him was worrisome. "Are you flirting with me, Noah?"

"Would that be a bad thing?"

"Let me count the ways." Gwen set her empty bowl beside his. Her gaze took in the establishment's shabby chic décor, dark wood paneling and deep red accents. "If I decide to run for office, we'd have to keep our relationship professional."

"Of course." But his eyes reminded her that they weren't working together yet.

"We're still very different, Noah. I'm an advocate who believes in public service. You believe in money."

Their server appeared at the table with their entrées. Gwen had requested the blackened tuna and asparagus. The aroma of the spicy seasonings made her mouth water. Noah had chosen the blackened chicken with loaded baked potato. Chances were good they'd both fall asleep at their desks later this afternoon.

Noah picked up their discussion once the server had left. "Even politicians should be fairly compensated for their work."

"I'm not talking about political salaries. I'm talking about policies that pander to the wealthy at the expense of the poor and middle class. To paraphrase Doctor King, the policies that take necessities from the masses to increase luxuries for the classes."

"I don't support those policies anymore." Noah had the grace to look ashamed.

"Oh, come on, Noah." Gwen had a vague memory of a similar disagreement with Noah thirty-one years ago, shortly before they broke off their relationship. "You and most, if not all, of your associates believe there should be winners and losers. What you don't seem to understand is that the options aren't 'win or lose.' The options are 'life and death.'"

"I understand that now." Noah paused with his silverware in his hands. "But we don't have to agree on policies to be able to run an effective campaign."

"I disagree with that." Gwen returned to her food, but with only half of her appetite. The rest of it was in tatters around the table.

"I haven't agreed with every policy idea my clients have."

"Then how could you work for them?"

"Do you agree with every policy of the candidate you vote for?"

"No, I don't." Gwen sighed. "This is a lot to consider."

"You're right. We've dropped a bombshell on you. I understand you'll need to think this over, and even discuss it with your husband and family."

"I'm divorced." Gwen noticed a slight shift in Noah's expression. Relief? Interest?

"I'm sorry."

"I'm not." Gwen tilted her head. "What about you?"

A cloud drifted across his eyes. "My wife died thirteen years ago."

"I'm so sorry. Had she been ill?"

"No." Noah seemed to push through sad memories. "You once said that I'd led a charmed life and that was one of the reasons I couldn't empathize with people who'd had to overcome tragedies and other struggles. Maybe you were right. After my wife died, I changed my position on a lot of policies."

Gwen had additional questions but sensed this wasn't the time. "I'll need time to think this over."

"Of course. We're tight on time, though. Let us know as soon as you can."

"I'll have a decision by next week. Maybe sooner." Act in haste, repent at leisure. Why did she have the sense that this campaign would give her a lot of reasons to repent? "I'm concerned that I may be too far out of my element. Maybe my time and resources would be better served helping my neighbors gain a voice in the capital rather than campaigning."

Noah leaned into the booth table. "Gwen, if you win this election, *you* would be that voice at the capital for your neighbors."

The idea had appeal, but what if she didn't get elected?

***

Gwen had created a mini oasis in her foyer in front of her new walnut wood bookcase. After eating the lentil soup she'd packed for lunch as her light dinner Wednesday evening, she'd curled up on her new black-and-white fluffy cloth armchair and called her children. She'd already spoken with her son, Andrew "Drew" Taylor Gaston. Now she was waiting to broach the subject with her daughter, Margaret "Maggie" Taylor Gaston.

The twenty-four-year-old was a grant writer for a nonprofit organization based in Philadelphia. Her little girl had flown far from the nest, just like her older brother. Drew was a finance director for a New York-based nonprofit group. Drew and Maggie called her every day, but she still missed them. Why had she raised her children to be so independent? Gwen pressed the cell phone closer to her ear and refocused on her daughter's conversation.

"But enough about me, Mom." Maggie's voice bounced with the energy and optimism of youth. "What's new and exciting in your world?"

Gwen hesitated. "I do have some interesting news."

"What is it?"

Gwen imagined her daughter sitting cross-legged on her mattress in the bedroom of the apartment she shared with two other women. She'd probably freed her thick cloud of dark brown hair from a conservative bun and changed from business casual to gray sweats.

"Cynthia and Kenneth asked me to consider running against our incumbent state senator, Dexter Jackson." Gwen listened hard for Maggie's reaction. She didn't have long to wait.

Maggie gasped. "You're running for state senate?"

"I don't know yet. I'm still thinking about it." Gwen rushed to put the brakes on her daughter's enthusiasm. Maggie had her going from considering running to launching a full-fledged campaign in less than thirty seconds.

"What's to think about, Mom? You're a natural leader." In typical Maggie fashion, her daughter steamrolled over Gwen's doubts.

"I've never held public office before." Gwen unwrapped herself from her armchair and wandered her foyer. Her stocking feet were silent on her polished Maplewood flooring. "How do you know?"

"Because you have what it takes. You're well-informed, probably better informed than a lot of the bozos in office." The sounds in the background implied Maggie had climbed off her bed and was pacing her bedroom. Like mother, like daughter. "You're also a great listener. Once they're elected, our public servants stop listening to us. They only have time for their big-money donors, but you listen because you really care."

"Being a public servant means that I'll be open to scrutiny, and not just me. The media will pry into your life and Drew's life as well." The idea of losing her privacy made Gwen uncomfortable. The thought of people going after her children made Gwen see red.

"Let them." Maggie spoke with a shrug in her voice. "I don't have anything to hide, and Drew's the original Mister Squeaky-Clean."

"That's true."

She'd been blessed with her children. They'd never given her cause to worry. Except that time Maggie borrowed her car without permission – and without a license. And then there was the time that Drew broke curfew and Gwen was getting ready to call all the hospitals. The memory made her think of Trayvon Martin. Gwen relived the fear she'd felt that night. It once again shook her to the core. What kind of horror were Travyon Martin's parents living through while their child's murderer walked free? Gwen stumbled back to her armchair.

"What did Drew say?" Maggie's question rescued Gwen from the darkness.

"He said the same things you're saying." Gwen's voice was still unsteady.

Drew was more cautious than Maggie. Gwen had been sure her son would talk her out of running for public office. She'd been wrong. To have the support and encouragement of both of her children was overwhelming.

"That settles it, then," Maggie announced. "What can we do to help?"

Gwen held up a hand even though Maggie couldn't see her. "Wait a minute. I haven't decided whether I'm running."

"What's holding you back, Mom?" Maggie sounded genuinely confused.

Gwen massaged her forehead with the tips of her left fingers. "I'm supposed to be retiring, remember? Not planning for a second career. I bought an armchair with an ottoman and a bookcase-"

"Yes, yes, and you were going to spend the rest of your life sleeping, reading and occasionally eating. There's only one thing that's really wrong with your plan, Mom."

"What's that?"

"No one believes you." Maggie laughed. "You're too civically active. You've been that way my whole life. You were probably that way even before you had Drew and me."

Gwen stared blindly across the room. "I don't know, Mags. This is a big step, and the campaign will change our lives forever."

"I know." Maggie's voice was a gentle murmur. "If you're worried about Drew and me, don't be. We support you. If you're worried about yourself, don't be. Drew and I will love you forever."

"I love you both so much."

"And, hey, you're always talking about Drew and me moving back home. If you make it to the White House, we will."

Chapter 4

"Why does Leap Day always feel like an extra day of work?" Clark's sigh was weighted with disgust.

"Because it is." Seated on the other side of the restaurant's booth table, Noah's gaze moved away from his youngest son. His smile faded. The dinner crowd was multiplying. "I left a message inviting James to join us. I guess he's not coming."

Clark looked empathetic. "You know, Dad, you don't have to bribe him with food. Save your money and just go talk to him."

"I've tried that." Noah returned his attention to the restaurant's menu. "I never make it past the door."

"Ouch."

That summed it up. The scents of seasoned meat, heavy sauces and sautéed vegetables should have stirred his appetite. They didn't. Noah set aside his menu. He couldn't concentrate on the words on the pages. When their server took their order, he'd trust his instincts.

"How was work?"

Clark's shoulders moved in a restless gesture. "The usual, and then I updated the agency's malware protection."

Noah grimaced. His son sounded bored. "Did you get a chance to work on your computer game program during your lunch hour?"

Clark's expression lit with excitement. Noah grinned as his son dove into an update of his dream project: the programming challenges he'd resolved, the ones he was still thinking through, the story plot schemes he was developing. Noah felt the waves of enthusiasm rolling across their table. He gave himself a mental pat on the back for his increasing understanding of his son's work. At first, he'd understood every tenth word. Today, he understood every seventh word. Great strides.

His son's passion for his computer game program carried them through their ordering dinner and the delivery of their entrees. This is what Noah had wanted for his children. He believed the old adage that, if you loved your career, you wouldn't work a day in your life.

Clark's enthusiasm reminded Noah of himself when he'd first started working on election campaigns. He'd loved every minute of every campaign. He'd thrown himself into each experience without regret. But during the past few campaigns he'd worked for, he'd felt more like an enabler than a champion. Noah was confident he could reclaim his passion for his work – with the right candidate. Something told him that Gwen was that candidate. He hadn't agreed with all of her past progressive ideas, but he believed in her passion and compassion for her community.

Clark came up for air. "So how was your day?"

Noah hesitated. "It was interesting. I offered to run the campaign of the candidate who's considering challenging Dexter Jackson."

Clark paused mid-chew before swallowing a bite of his steak. "You're going to support your former client's opposition? Who is he?"

"She. Gwen Taylor."

"I've never heard of her."

"She's the director of the Metropolitan Public Library and a member of a community social justice group." Noah's explanation didn't appear to clear Clark's confusion.

Clark spread his hands. He held his knife in one and his fork in the other. "You're going to manage the campaign of a person who's never run for public office and doesn't have any name recognition against a well-known incumbent for a state senate seat with the primary just three months away? Why would you do that to yourself?"

Noah's iced tea glass was cold against his palm. "The fact that she's not a politician is one of the reasons I'm interested in running her campaign. It'll be an exciting challenge."

"It'll be a challenge all right."

Noah sliced into his steak, releasing the scents of black pepper, kosher salt, garlic, onions and coriander that seasoned the well-done meat. "Gwen's assertive, passionate and sincere. She'll attract support because her goals are based on the issues that matter to the people in our community. Voters will connect with her because they'll see themselves in her."

Clark was silent for several thought-filled moments. "Is she pretty?"

Noah's discomfort was inexplicable and uncalled for. Just as inexplicable and uncalled for as his relief at learning Gwen was unmarried.

"She is. She's also an ex-girlfriend." Noah waited until Clark stopped coughing. His root beer must have gone down his windpipe. "We dated in our twenties, before I met your mother."

Clark dried his eyes. "If the media finds out about your past, they'll zero in on *that* instead of Ms. Taylor's campaign message."

"You're right." Noah acknowledged Clark's point. A rekindled romance between a campaign manager and a candidate would be a sexier talking point than a community oversight board to review policing practices.

"You must really admire her." Clark dug into his loaded baked potato. "You should ask her out if she decides not to run. If she does run, you should probably keep your distance."

"I can handle it." And if he repeated that often enough, maybe he'd believe it.

***

"You seem deep in thought this morning." Edwina sank onto one of Gwen's visitor's chairs early Thursday morning. "What's on your mind?"

Gwen took a breath, drawing in the scent of her dark roast coffee and its French vanilla creamer. It was chilly in her office. The hot java warmed her from the inside out. She'd barely slept last night. Like sugar plums on the night before Christmas, visions of election campaigns had danced in her head.

"Cynthia and Kenneth came by yesterday afternoon. They brought Senator Jackson's former campaign manager, Noah Barrow, with them."

Edwina's dark brown eyes expressed both surprise and curiosity. "Your ex-boyfriend? Why did they stop by?"

Gwen ignored Edwina's reference to her past. "They want me to challenge Senator Jackson in the primary. Noah's left the senator's campaign and he's offered to run mine."

Edwina clapped her hands in excitement. Her heart-shaped face glowed with enthusiasm. "That's wonderful! I should have thought of that. You'd be perfect. What can I do to help?"

Gwen blinked. Had she stepped into an alternate dimension? What other explanation could there be for her best friends and her children losing their collective minds over the possibility of her campaign? "Edwina, I haven't decided whether I'm going to campaign."

"Of course you should campaign." Edwina's expression dimmed with confusion. "You know the district. You're well-versed on the issues. You have viable solutions."

Gwen's thoughts tumbled over themselves. "All of what you've just said is true, and of course I'm interested. This would be a chance for me to advance our causes myself. But, Edwina, there are so many reasons why I'm *not* a qualified candidate."

Edwina sat back, and crossed her arms and legs. "Give me one."

Gwen considered her friend's stubborn expression, and her deceptively conservative emerald blazer, cream shell and tailored black pants. "I don't have the slightest idea of how to run a campaign. That lack of knowledge alone could end our experiment as soon as it begins."

"Noah does and he's already offered to run yours, so that reason doesn't hold water." Edwina volleyed Gwen's objection back to her with the breathtaking speed of tennis pros Venus and Serena Williams. "I researched his background. He has decades of experience running successful campaigns, which means he'll be able to give you great advice. It also means he has tons of contacts. And – bonus! – his contacts have deep pockets. He'll be able to help bring in campaign money. Next."

Gwen acknowledged Edwina's point, but … "I don't have any experience serving in public office."

"Neither does our current state senator." Edwina uncrossed her arms and legs, leaning forward. "We're librarians. We have advanced degrees in research. You're also exceptionally smart. The fact is that our community needs people like you, Gwen. People who sincerely care."

Gwen considered her friend. "Edwina, why don't *you* run for office?"

Edwina shook her head, causing her wavy dark brown hair to swing around her shoulders. "You're the problem solver, and that's another thing that our community needs: People who can identify problems, come up with solutions and put in the work to make things happen."

Gwen took another drink of her coffee. The strong roast blend sent a welcomed jolt through her groggy system. "I'm a newbie without name recognition running against a two-term incumbent. Once the media exposes those facts, my campaign will shut down."

"The community needs change. Show them that you're that change and this time next year, you could be sworn into office." Edwina cocked her head. "What did Drew and Maggie say?"

Gwen smiled. Her friend knew her so well. "They're excited by the idea of my running for office. I wanted to speak with them first, which is the reason I didn't say anything to you yesterday."

"I understand." Edwina nodded. "It's settled then. Our community deserves better representation. Drew, Maggie, Cynthia, Kenneth and I – and even Noah – think you're the right person for the job."

"I wish I did." Gwen rose to pace her office. "I'm sick and tired of calling our public servants to ask them to address gun safety or racial profiling or the school-to-prison pipeline or... insert issue here... only to be given a pat on the head before they completely ignore me."

"Then run for office." Edwina shifted on her chair to face Gwen. "Instead of waiting for the invitation to the table, you'll already have a seat."

"You're right." Suddenly, Gwen was energized by a thought she'd never allowed to take form. "These issues that we're dealing with – stop-and-frisk, school funding, infrastructure improvements – are not just local issues. They should be addressed at the state and national levels."

Edwina pointed at her. "And *you* can do that once you're in office."

Gwen ignored the tremor of fear causing her muscles to quake. "All right. I'll challenge Senator Jackson for his state senate seat." She marched back to her desk and dropped onto her chair. Gwen tugged her purse from her bottom desk drawer and fished out Noah's business card. "But first, I'll make sure Noah's still willing to manage my campaign."

Edwina stood. "If he's not available, we'll find someone else. The important thing is that we're getting a representative who'll actually represent us."

Gwen held up a hand. "*If* I win."

"Oh, you'll win. I have no doubt about that." Edwina tossed her a smile before breezing out of the office.

"Humph. No pressure," Gwen muttered under her breath. Her fingers shook as she dialed Noah's number. He answered on the second ring.

"Noah Barrow."

Gwen's heart fluttered. She wasn't certain that it was just nerves. "It's Gwen. Are you still willing to manage my campaign?"

***

"What am I supposed to do on social media?" Gwen studied the task list that lay on the table in front of her Thursday evening. There was so much to do.

Noah had given the list to her about ten minutes ago when they'd first sat at the small, circular ash wood conversation desk in a corner of his office.

It was almost seven P.M. but members of Noah's staff also were working late. The echo of computer keys, snippets of murmured conversations and the occasional burst of spontaneous laughter floated through Noah's open door. Those reminders that they weren't alone in the suite kept their meeting from feeling intimate.

"We'll use Twitter, Facebook and Pinterest to support and reinforce our campaign messages. Keep pushing those messages out until our constituents can recite them in their sleep." Noah sounded confident and in charge as he reviewed the steps they'd have to take to get her campaign off the ground.

Gwen's eyes threatened to cross as she studied the task list: election filings, media interviews, fund-raisers, public appearances, social media platforms, on and on. And on.

What had she gotten herself into? Should she reconsider? She was second guessing herself. And third guessing, and fourth guessing. Gwen slid a look toward Noah. The first task on their to-do list should be picking her up off the ground in the event she fainted.

Get a grip, Taylor.

Gwen had grabbed a quick dinner with Edwina before driving to Noah's office. Edwina had been just as excited as Cynthia and Kenneth had been when she'd learned that Gwen was meeting with Noah that night. After a hectic day, however, Gwen's sleepless night was catching up with her. Maybe that was the reason she felt so overwhelmed. Or maybe this new opportunity was just that overwhelming.

"How does anyone make the decision to run for public office when there are so many hoops to jump through?"

Noah gave her an encouraging look. "Just remember that you're not doing this alone."

Gwen took a steadying breath. For now, she'd focus only on the task they were addressing. She'd ignore the rest. "I'm not on social media."

The library had various social media platforms and an electronic newsletter to communicate with patrons and donors, but Gwen didn't use the applications. Her only role in the process was to approve the messages and images before they were posted.

"I'll help you set up your accounts and my team will help grow your followers." Noah sounded reassuring.

"You've mentioned your team a couple of times." Gwen lifted her gaze, surprised to find Noah studying her. "Since I suppose they're also my team now, I'd like to meet them."

"You will. Tomorrow. Although we're a small group, I didn't want to distract you with introductions tonight. I wanted to focus on the process, which you noticed could be overwhelming." Noah lowered his electronic tablet to his desk and sat back. "Sandy Weaks runs our office. Stu Meyer coordinates our volunteers. Yao Fang is our fund-raising director, although Cynthia's also interested in bringing in donors."

"Good. Since I'm not the party's candidate, I'll need help raising money to pay you and our team."

"We won't have trouble bringing in money." Noah flashed a smile. Gwen wished for a tenth of his confidence. "Mary Abala is our finance chair and Emma Templeton manages our grassroots efforts. Don't call her E.T., though. She doesn't like it."

Gwen blinked. "It would never have crossed my mind to do that."

Noah's eyes lingered on her face. His gaze was like a physical caress before he returned to their launch list. "We'll also have to do a full background check on you: personal and professional histories, family members alive and deceased, finances, etcetera."

Could she handle this level of invasion to her privacy? Gwen shifted on her chair. "Is that necessary?"

Noah gave her an understanding look. "We need a comprehensive report of your background up to present day so we can identify any weaknesses Dexter will exploit. We don't want to be caught off guard. That would put our campaign on the defensive and distract from our message. For example, tax evasion."

"I pay my taxes." Gwen was offended.

"Fraud."

"I've never broken the law."

"Parking tickets."

"All right, so I've broken a few." She could feel her cheeks heating. How deep will this investigation go: school grades, library fines, cavities? "How long will this background check take and what do you need from me to get it started?"

"I know a guy. I've worked with him before. He's thorough and he's quick." Noah paused to make a note on his tablet before turning his attention back to Gwen. "I've done some preliminary research on you."

"You did?" Shock wiped her mind blank.

"Of course." Noah gave her the half smile that curled her toes. It reminded her of their late-night political debates, long walks in the park and Teddy Pendergrass's "Love T.K.O." "I'm not going to offer to manage someone's political campaign without first checking what I was getting into."

Gwen had better get used to the scrutiny if she wanted to serve in public office. "Did you find anything that would be problematic?"

"I found I was very interested in running your campaign." Noah grew serious. "Dexter doesn't have a message. He's running on his record, which we both know hasn't always benefitted the majority of his constituents. So I can't stress this enough: Whatever we do, we have to stay on message."

"I agree." Gwen's throat went dry. Noah's intensity was very appealing. "The worst thing I could think of that's in my past is my ex-husband."

Noah's midnight eyes sharpened on hers. "Why is he the worst thing?"

"Divorce is never pleasant."

"Whose idea was the divorce?"

"It was mine." Gwen felt the usual spurt of defensiveness. Failure wasn't something she was used to, and her marriage had been a doozy.

"Why?" Noah's eyes held only interest; no judgement.

Gwen hesitated. "He'd been unfaithful." Noah's compassionate listening had Gwen sharing more than she'd intended, more than she'd shared with even Edwina and Cynthia. "I'd confronted him as soon as I'd found out. He tried to lie, but I wouldn't let him. He promised never to be unfaithful again, but I didn't believe him. I think a part of me was afraid that if I forgave him that first time, we'd end up in a pattern of him cheating and me forgiving him. Pretty soon, I'd hate myself even more than I'd hate him, and I didn't want that for myself or my children."

"Now I know that I'm looking at our next state senator." Noah's quiet words surprised Gwen.

"How do you know?"

"You've proven that you can make the difficult decisions even when you're faced with tough personal choices. That's the kind of leadership we need in government."

For the first time since getting on this crazy ride, Gwen felt optimistic. Noah knew a lot about politics and politicians. If he believed Gwen had what it took to hold public office, then she could believe it, too.

"I hope I can convey that to voters in time for the June primary."

"You will." Noah spread his hands. "You have my vote."

Gwen smiled. "That's a start."

CHAPTER 5

"I thought you said you'd never used social media before?" Noah watched in surprise late Saturday morning as Gwen's fingers moved quickly and surely over the keyboard. She navigated the Facebook screen to upload the professional photo they'd taken of her that morning and type in the brief biography they'd crafted.

They were once again meeting in Noah's office. It was the first Saturday of March. Noah had wanted Gwen to be comfortable with the social media tools in the event she wanted to upload messages herself. Gwen sat at his desk using his laptop. Noah was seated close beside her. Close enough to feel her warmth. Close enough to smell the soap on her skin and, just beneath it, lavender. Her scent brought back memories of late-night political debates, takeout pizza and The Commodores's "You Bring Me Up."

Gwen slipped him a teasing look. Her moist, bow-shaped lips curved into a smile. "In preparation for our meeting today, I read up on Facebook, Twitter and Pinterest. I also spoke with the person who manages our library system's social media programs."

"You were always well-prepared. Getting to know you again, I'm even more committed to your campaign."

After Joyce's death, Noah had never thought he'd feel this heady sense of attraction again. And that had been fine. Being a father gave Noah a reason to get out of bed. It gave him a sense of pride and belonging. And love. And that had been enough. But now that he'd reconnected with Gwen, he realized how much he'd missed that rush of energy and excitement to see a certain person. It was different from the feelings he'd had with Joyce, but it was just as special.

There was still so much of the younger Gwen in the woman seated beside him. The old memories were making him restless.

Gwen's cinnamon-tinged cheeks grew pink. "Hopefully, the majority of voting constituents will feel the way you do."

Noah would do everything in his power to make certain of that. "We need to get you in front of them through newspapers, radio, television and personal appearances." He gestured toward the computer monitor. "And social media."

Gwen returned her attention to her Facebook profile. "This campaign is going to be expensive."

"Donations will come in once it's established. Cynthia and Kenneth have already offered to host a fund-raiser. They have a lot of wealthy connections. I know a few people, too."

Gwen's laughter rolled down Noah's spine. "You're very modest. You know all of the movers and shakers in the state. That's probably one of the reasons you have such a high success rate."

"Is that the reason you asked me to manage your campaign?" Her answer mattered perhaps too much. But what did he expect her to say?

What did he *want* her to say?

Of course she'd want someone experienced and connected to manage her campaign whether it was her first venture or her eightieth. But did he want her to say that their shared past had factored into her decision?

Was Clark right? Was he backing Gwen's candidacy because he was still attracted to his former girlfriend?

Gwen laughed again, causing the muscles in Noah's lower abdomen to tangle. "It's not the only reason. I admire your integrity."

Sex appeal would have been nice, but he'd settle for *integrity*. "Thank you."

"Your withdrawal from Senator Jackson's campaign rather than giving in to his decision to run a smear campaign impressed me." Gwen's warm cocoa eyes hypnotized Noah. "The younger Noah would not have done that. He had more of a win-at-all-costs attitude."

Noah looked away. "I've done some growing up over the past thirty-one years."

Gwen finally broke the uncomfortable silence. "It's your turn. You offered to work with me before I'd even decided to challenge Senator Jackson for his seat. Why?"

Because you're one of the most fascinating, captivating, intelligent women – people – I've ever met. But those fourteen words could end their association before their campaign even launched. "You impress me. You've always impressed me. You're smart, tough, passionate and persistent. You'll need all of those qualities to make it in the public sector. I also spoke with Cynthia and Kenneth who speak very highly of you. They put me in touch with other associates – your neighbors and members of your church – who can't say enough good things about you. They're excited to help with your campaign."

"That's good because I'm going to need all of the help that I can get." Gwen returned her attention to her social media account.

Noah considered the perfect posture of her dancer's figure, the shiny raven tresses with hints of gray that balanced on her shoulders, the lavender scent that lingered in the air. Gwen wasn't the only one who'd need a lot of help. In his mind, Prince played an encore of "I Want to be Your Lover."

***

"That was fast." Noah led his friend and private investigator, Foster Capehart, into his office late Thursday morning. It was the third week of March.

His friend's six-foot-five-inch frame was clothed in another standard black outfit. Today, it was a black knit sweater, black jeans and black hiking boots. After their four-year association, Noah had concluded that Foster didn't have any other colors in his clothing repertoire.

Maybe the dark attire was his agency's branding. It added to his intimidation. Foster reminded Noah – and probably everyone he met – of a granite mountain. The sharp angles of his broad dark face coupled with his piercing onyx eyes dispelled any idea that the investigator had a softer side.

Foster folded his long, muscled frame onto one of Noah's two guest chairs. He pinned Noah with a cold look. "Are you playing me?"

His long-time friend's unexpected attack disconcerted Noah. "No. Why?"

"Is Gwendolyn Catherine Taylor real?"

"Very. Why?"

Foster didn't seem convinced. "She's so clean she squeaks. She's what she seems: hardworking city employee, dedicated mom, social justice activist. No suspicious activities. No weird memberships. That's why the search went fast. There was nothing for me to dig into."

Noah heard the concern in Foster's voice. "That's good news, isn't it?"

"It's unreal." Foster propped his right ankle on his left knee and continued to watch Noah closely. He balanced a nine-by-twelve black envelope on his right thigh. "I've never had such clean results on a background check. You say she's a budding politician?"

"That's right."

Foster was already shaking his clean-shaven head. "Does she know what she's in for? A political campaign will chew someone like her up and spit her out. Her opponents will eat her alive. Hell, her allies will eat her alive."

"I don't think so." Noah was amused. A memory of his first meeting with Gwen at an Equal Rights Amendment rally in 1981 came to mind. She'd introduced herself by taking him to task on his lack of knowledge on the issues. "On paper, Gwen may appear to be a mild-mannered librarian, but people who cross her will find she has a very tough alter ego."

"If you say so." Foster shrugged his thick dark eyebrows. He leaned forward to pass Noah the thin black envelope, which contained Foster's report on Gwen's background check.

Noah pulled the bound report from the envelope. "You're certain that Gwen's files are clean?"

"She's probably cleaner than you." Foster linked his fingers together in front of his flat stomach. His reputation supported his confidence in his work. "If *I* couldn't find anything on her, no one will. No record. Not even unpaid parking tickets. She files her taxes and pays her credit cards in their entirety and on time."

"That's what I like to hear." His client continued to impress him.

"Her parents are another story."

Noah looked up, giving Foster a sharp look. His friend's expression gave nothing away. "What did you learn?"

"I had to do a deeper dive into them. Eustace and Macy Taylor came to the United States from the Dominican Republic illegally in 1956."

Noah's stomach dropped. "What?"

"But," Foster raised his voice to be heard over Noah. "They received their citizenship in 1991."

"That's a relief." But had the crisis been averted?

Foster gave a rare smile. "They filed for their citizenship after then-President Ronald Reagan signed his version of the citizenship amnesty program, the Immigration Reform and Control Act of 1986."

Noah inclined his head. "That act granted legal status to - what was it? Three million immigrants?"

"Two-point-seven million people who'd entered the country before 1982," Foster corrected him. "I looked it up. Estimates are that a third of those people became naturalized citizens by 2001, including Gwen's parents."

Noah skipped forward in the report to the section that summarized Foster's research into Gwen's parents. He skimmed the text. "This means that Gwen's parents were here illegally when I met her in nineteen-eighty-one. Why hadn't she told me?"

Over the past three weeks, they'd spent every evening together as well as much of the weekends. They researched the issues she planned to address and worked on her messaging. In fact, they'd spent so much time together that Gwen's lavender scent had started following Noah to bed.

Foster shrugged. "Ask her."

"I'll do that after our press interview tonight." Noah rubbed the back of his neck. "How much of a problem will this be for Gwen's campaign?"

Foster shrugged again. "You know Dexter. What'll he do?"

Noah didn't have to consider his answer. "His attack will focus on Gwen's parents entering the United States illegally. He'll leave out the parts about her parents being approved for amnesty under Reagan's act or that they earned their citizenship."

Foster gestured toward his report, which remained open on Noah's desk. "They were model citizens just like their daughter. Her mother was a cook in a small Caribbean restaurant. Her father worked in construction. They volunteered in their community, paid their rent on time, and raised a great kid."

"Yes, they did." Noah glanced down at the report. "We'll have to work that story line into her messaging and frame her parents as role models."

"You're the expert." Foster stood, calling an end to their meeting. "Your bill's in the mail."

Noah watched his pragmatic friend escort himself from the office before returning to the report. What else would he find here?

Chapter 6

Gwen was crashing toward panic. She was stiff in the chair beside Noah Thursday evening. What were those talking points they'd reviewed? Her mind was blank.

Trevor Hollis, a reporter with *The Daily*, confronted her from the opposite side of the glass-and-metal rectangular conference table. "So, let me see if I've got this straight. *You're* going to challenge State Senator Dexter Jackson, the *incumbent* of your own party?"

Panic made a sharp turn toward aggravation. Was the reporter sleepwalking through the interview? The recent college graduate's dark brown hair was disheveled. So was his beige and tan clothing. His gray eyes were bloodshot, and he was sporting a wicked five o'clock shadow.

"That's right." Gwen worked to compose her voice. "We need public servants who will actually serve the public. Senator Jackson has stopped listening to us. I'm prepared to bring our voices directly to our state government."

Trevor pointed toward Noah. "Aren't you the senator's campaign manager?" Finally, a flicker of interest entered the reporter's sleepy gray eyes.

"I've resigned from Senator Jackson's campaign." Noah's casual demeanor seemed forced. "I'm fully committed to Gwen Taylor's platform of public service and inclusivity."

Gwen winced. There was so much more to her messages. Reducing them to ten-second sound bites made her ideas appear inane and disingenuous.

Awake now, Trevor scribbled feverishly in his reporter's notebook. "Did you resign from Senator Jackson's campaign or did he fire you? If you resigned, why? Same question if he fired you."

Gwen's heart sank. They'd lost control of the interview. Her mind raced to find a way to salvage the situation. She drew a deep breath – and was temporarily distracted by Noah's soap-and-mint scent.

Noah spoke as though the reporter had also strained his patience. "Senator Jackson and I disagreed on how to run his campaign. When I learned that Gwen was interested in running for office, I was quick to offer her my services."

Noah made a valiant effort to turn the subject back to Gwen and her campaign, but the reporter didn't bite. Trevor had found a shinier object: Noah and Dexter's breakup. Gwen winced as she imagined the potential headline: Jackson's Campaign Manager Dumps Senator for No-Name Challenger.

Trevor continued scribbling into his notebook. "What was the difference of opinion about?"

"I'm not part of Senator Jackson's campaign any longer." Noah leaned into the conference table, folding his large hands on its wide glass surface. "We invited you here to discuss Gwen Taylor's campaign and the issues she's championing."

Trevor nodded as he continued to take notes. "Does Senator Jackson know that you're working for the woman who's going to challenge him in the primaries?"

The reporter's follow-up question indicated that the prospect of pitting Noah against the senator was worth the risk of a blown interview.

Gwen stifled a sigh. "I'm grateful for Mr. Barrow's support of my campaign. If I'm elected to the state senate, I'll work to end stop-and-frisk, establish greater oversight of community policing, enforce common sense gun control measures and for further improvements to the Affordable Care Act."

Trevor didn't transcribe a single syllable of her words. Instead he'd used her impassioned declaration as a timeout to stretch his fingers. Gwen was dumbstruck.

Trevor pointed again toward Noah. "How do you think Dexter Jackson will react when he learns that you're managing his opponent's campaign?"

Noah stood. His movements were stiff with annoyance. "This interview's over."

Trevor stammered. "But we've only just started."

"You're wasting our time." Noah held the younger man's startled gaze. "You're more interested in my leaving Senator Jackson's campaign than in Gwen Taylor's platform and the issues your readers will be voting on in the June primary."

Noah looked at Gwen. She saw the apology in his eyes and hoped her nod of approval absolved him of any guilt. She was relieved that he'd terminated the reporter's sham interview.

Trevor pushed off his seat. He still seemed disconcerted as he collected his notebook and pen. "I only have one or two other questions about the senator, then I'm absolutely interested in whatever you want to tell me about Gwen Taylor. Deal?"

"No deal." Noah spoke over his shoulder. He crossed the room to hold the door open for the reporter. "Address your questions about Senator Jackson to the senator and his team. When you're ready to talk about Gwen Taylor's campaign, contact me to schedule an interview."

Gwen watched Trevor's stiff strides carry him out of the room. "That could have gone better."

Noah winced. "I'm sorry. I knew Trevor would be curious about my leaving Dexter's campaign. I hadn't expected him to make that the focus of our interview."

"We were both mistaken." The weight of Gwen's disappointment bore down on her as she rose from her chair. "I thought the media would be interested in a novice candidate primarying an incumbent. The media isn't interested in me or in my message."

"That was one reporter. He doesn't represent the entire media." Noah escorted Gwen from the conference room.

Gwen couldn't ignore the feel of Noah's palm at the small of her back no matter how she tried. His touch was warm and comforting through the emerald jacket of her pantsuit. "How do we draw attention away from Senator Jackson and his campaign?"

"By outworking him, and we will." Noah paused outside of his office, allowing Gwen to cross the threshold before him. "But first we have something other than media interviews to discuss."

Gwen turned to Noah. "That sounds foreboding."

Noah walked past her to his desk. "My investigator completed your background check."

Gwen took the binder Noah offered. "Have you read it?"

"Why didn't you tell me that your parents came to the United States illegally?"

Gwen would take Noah's response as a yes, he had read the report. His question caught her off guard. So did his reaction. Noah seemed hurt. "They earned their citizenship in-"

"I know." Noah shoved his hands into his front pants pockets. "But I don't understand why you didn't tell me."

"We knew each other for less than a year, Noah." Gwen paced away from him in irritation. She snatched her handbag and her winter coat from the black wooden coatrack in the far corner of his office. "And your position on immigration was pretty clear - and obviously based on everything *but* the facts."

"My views on immigration have evolved." Noah circled his desk to help Gwen with her coat.

Gwen arched an eyebrow at Noah from over her shoulder. She was close enough to see the dark brown and gray hairs that formed his faint five o'clock shadow. Close enough to touch them. "What caused this evolution?"

"Not what, who." Noah dropped his hands from Gwen's coat and stepped around to stand in front of her. "You left an impression on me. It didn't happen overnight, but you challenged me to find answers on my own rather than blindly follow any party's platform."

The fight drained from Gwen and another type of tension took hold. She stepped back, putting more distance between them.

"You've changed a lot in the past three decades."

A shadow flickered across Noah's angular features. "More than you know."

Gwen felt the sadness reflected in Noah's eyes. She sensed his grief was caused by more than the death of his beloved wife. What other sorrows had touched him?

***

Gwen turned up the volume on the small black radio she kept on her desk. It wasn't quite eleven o'clock Friday morning. The anchor on the local National Public Radio station had just mentioned President Barack Obama.

"While in the Rose Garden this morning to announce his nominee for president of the World Bank, President Obama was asked for his thoughts on the murder of seventeen-year-old Trayvon Martin."

A movement in her peripheral vision drew Gwen's attention. Edwina stood in her office doorway. Gwen waved her in.

Meanwhile, the anchor continued her report. "Martin was killed the night of Sunday, February twenty-sixth in Sanford, Florida, by gunman George Zimmerman while Martin was walking home after purchasing candy and soda from a neighborhood convenience store."

"Could you turn it up more?" Edwina whispered as she settled onto one of the chairs. Gwen boosted the volume.

President Obama's voice came clearly through the radio. "If I had a son, he'd look like Trayvon."

The words tore at Gwen's heart. The president's grim tone gave voice to the pain and the fear with which she, Edwina and countless millions of other people across the country were struggling. This senseless murder of an unarmed child filled her with breathtaking anger and heartbreaking sorrow. She could only imagine the anguish young Trayvon's parents were going through. Gwen said another prayer for their strength and comfort.

President Obama continued. Pain edged his words. "All of us have to do some soul searching to figure out how does something like this happen. Obviously, this is a tragedy. I can only imagine what these parents are going through. When I think about this boy, I think about my own kids."

At the end of the report, Gwen turned off the radio. Her hands were shaking. "We both have grown children, but it doesn't matter that they're adults. It's their ethnicity, not their age, that makes them targets."

"I don't know what I'd do or how I'd respond if something like this happened to my child." Edwina's voice trembled. "But you don't have to be a parent to grieve for Trayvon, and his family and our community."

"And you don't have to be a genius to know that there's something very wrong with the fact that the Sanford police department initially declined to charge his murderer."

"This could not have been what Florida's stand your ground law was intended for."

Gwen pressed a palm against her uneasy stomach. "It's hard not to feel like live targets in our own communities. In our homes. On our streets. Rational people would have thought that after high-profile cases like Amadou Diallo's and Abner Louima's, our government at all levels would have taken action to ensure civilians were better protected."

In New York City in 1997, Abner Louima had been assaulted, brutalized and forcibly sodomized by police officers. Two years later, Amadou Diallo was shot and killed by four New York City plain-clothed police officers. Neither man had been armed, nor had they posed any threat. The nation's newspapers, radio stations and television broadcasts covered the crisis for a few weeks, then unceremoniously returned to their status quo, allowing such outrages by law enforcement and vigilantes to be repeated, often without much, if any, news coverage.

"The media works hard to vilify the victims." Edwina crossed her arms and legs. "All cops and vigilantes have to say is, 'I feared for my life.'"

Gwen shared the disgust she felt rolling off her friend in waves. "The National Rifle Association throws the second amendment in a lockbox as though real lives don't matter, and people talk about 'healing in the community.' We're past healing.

We need our public servants to stop protecting guns and start protecting people."

"How do we get them to start listening to we the people instead of their campaign donors?" Edwina's tone was tight with anger.

Gwen picked up her pen, rolling the hard plastic between the thumb and first two fingers of her right hand. "Trayvon Martin's murder makes me even more anxious to get into public office so that I can work for stronger justice reforms."

"Your campaign is picking up momentum. The local TV anchors were talking about your upcoming town hall meeting this morning, and I heard a news segment about you on the radio driving in."

In the three weeks since Gwen had been working with Noah on her campaign, they'd polished her message, scheduled events and recruited volunteers to deliver her campaign brochures door-to-door. Now newspapers, radio stations and television news producers were contacting her for interviews.

"My social media audience is growing." Which Gwen found only a *little* daunting. "I appreciate everything you're doing to help."

Edwina filled in for her when Gwen had campaign-related appointments. She'd also helped with follow-up calls to the media to press for even greater coverage of Gwen's campaign.

"I'm happy to do it." Edwina stood from her chair. "I hope we have record voter turnout in June."

"We'll see in a little more than ten weeks." Gwen's shoulder muscles tightened as she realized what she'd just said.

Ten weeks. Will the voters turn out for the primary? And if so, will they support her – or the status quo?

***

Visions of hamburgers taunted Noah as he sat at his desk. He thought he could smell a well-done Angus steak burger. It was after one o'clock Friday afternoon, but he had a report to finish before he left for lunch.

Noah tried to refocus his thoughts, but his cell phone's soft chime redirected his attention to his caller identification display. Dexter. Noah ignored the temptation not to take the call. "What can I do for you, Dexter?"

"Tell me you've come to your senses and will manage my campaign." Dexter's joviality was a ploy. Noah heard the express order in his words.

It didn't sway him. "I'm backing Gwen Taylor. You can ask me to come back to your campaign every day for the next ten weeks, Dexter. My answer will remain the same."

"You're pretending to manage her campaign because you want to teach me a lesson. It's not going to work. Stop wasting your time *and mine*, and get back to my campaign."

Noah detected some ambient noise on their connection. Did Dexter have him on speaker phone? Who else was in the room? Noah kept their potential audience in mind as he formulated his response.

"We've each made our choices." In the silence that followed his comment, Noah sensed Dexter's displeasure coming through the phone.

"You must think pretty highly of yourself."

"You must think highly of me, too, Dexter, since you keep trying to get me back on your campaign." Noah eased back against his chair. "Or maybe you're having trouble replacing me because I'm not the only campaign manager who doesn't want *you* managing *him*."

"Who says I'm having trouble replacing you?" Dexter barked the words.

"Why else would you keep calling?" Noah imagined his former client's face was darkening with an angry flush.

Dexter's short fuse was a warning sign Noah had tried to ignore. He shouldn't have. The senator's temper hadn't boded well for their working relationship much less for the incumbent's reelection. Not for the first time, Noah congratulated himself on leaving Dexter's campaign – and wondered why he'd ever accepted the job in the first place.

"Get this straight, Noah." Dexter seemed to be unraveling. "*I'm* doing *you* the favor."

"What makes you think that?"

"I'm trying to save your reputation." From the force in Dexter's voice, Noah guessed the senator was jabbing his stubby index finger toward the beige phone. "You should be backing a winner."

"I am." Noah interrupted Dexter's diatribe.

"What do you think prominent people in the community will think once they find out that you're backing some *nobody* from the local public library?"

It shocked Noah how quickly his temper ignited at Dexter's insult to Gwen. He clenched his fist around his cell phone and struggled to mask his anger. "Once the community hears Gwen's platform, they'll be more enthusiastic about the June primary. They'll be relieved that *you're* not their only option."

"I have experience."

"The people of this district need someone who can do more than sit on a chair."

There was another pause, this one deeper and more telling than the last. "It would be in your best interest to drop Gwen and return to my campaign."

Noah caught the threat in Dexter's statement. "Thanks for caring."

"You may not like playing games, Noah, but I'm willing to play hardball. Either you fall in line and return to my campaign or I'll leak damaging stories to the media."

It was harder for Noah to mask his anger this time. "I know that you want to smear Gwen. Unfortunately for you, she doesn't have any skeletons in her closet."

"No, she doesn't. She's a real goody-two-shoes. But can you say the same about yourself? Come back to my campaign or I'll open your closet to the media."

Noah saw red. Where did Dexter find the stones to threaten him? He could hear his teeth grinding. Feel the muscles in his neck tightening. Noah rose to pace across the thin gray carpet of his office. He stared blindly at the view from his seventh-floor office window. "Would you actually expect me to work for you after your threats?"

Dexter laughed. "Of course not. I wouldn't *want* you to work for me, either. After I got through with you, you'd be damaged goods. My point is, if I can't benefit from your expertise, neither can Gwen."

"I hear you, Dexter. Now *you* hear *me* because *this* is my final answer." Noah disconnected the call and returned to his desk.

Hopefully, this time Dexter would get the message that Noah wouldn't be dictated to. But Noah had a sinking feeling about Dexter's threat to expose Noah's past to the press. There was more at stake than Noah's pride. There was his sons' privacy.

And there was Gwen's trust.

Chapter 7

Gwen gripped her background report in her sweaty right hand. She considered Noah, seated on the other side of the small conference table in his office Friday evening. His thick amethyst sweater warmed his chocolate skin and made his midnight eyes look even darker. He was cool, confident, and completely in charge.

"I don't know whether I should feel reassured that there isn't anything in my past that Senator Jackson could use to smear me - or violated by how thorough this report is."

"I vote for reassured." Noah's deep voice rolled over her.

Gwen stiffened. Today was not the day to allow Noah's sex appeal to distract her. "We need to even the playing field. You know everything about me." She glanced at the report in her hand again. "It's only fair that I know more about you."

"I'm an open book." Noah spread his arms, inadvertently drawing Gwen's attention to his broad chest. "What would you like to know?"

She hesitated. "Tell me about your family."

Noah's smile faded. "You already know that my wife died. I have two sons. James is twenty-seven and a financial adviser with an investment company. Clark's twenty-two. He's a computer programmer with Metro University."

"I can hear how proud you are of them. I'm glad they're doing so well."

"Me, too." Noah seemed far away as he stared at the surface of the table between them. "Their mother would be also."

Noah seemed startled to have spoken the words aloud. His cloak of confidence had slipped, but he restored it effortlessly. Could he teach Gwen that trick?

"I'm so sorry that she isn't alive to see them for herself." Gwen hesitated. "May I ask her name?"

"Joyce. Joyce Ann Smith Barrow. She was born and raised in Texas. A lifelong Dallas Cowboys fan."

Gwen smiled through her grief for him. "That must have been hard for you to accept."

"As a lifelong Philadelphia Eagles fan, it was a struggle."

"I can believe it."

Noah cleared his throat. "The truth is, Gwen, Joyce didn't just die. She was murdered. Killed by a mass shooter. Our sons were only fourteen and nine at the time." He rubbed his face as though trying to remove the image from his eyes.

Gwen's breath caught in her throat. "Noah, I'm so very sorry."

"Joyce was visiting her family in Fort Worth. She was going to take Jim and Clark with her. At the last minute, she changed her mind. She and her family were at church. Church. Of all places."

Gwen's muscles tensed. The faded memory of a newspaper article came back to her. "Wedgewood Baptist Church?"

Noah nodded. "It changed my perspective on gun control legislation."

On September 15, 1999, a mass murderer killed seven members of the Wedgewood Baptist Church. Gwen's breath left her in a whoosh. She was so sorry for the tragedy. Sorry it had taken so many innocent lives, including Noah's wife. And sorry it had taken such a horrible heartbreak to change Noah's mind about sensible gun legislation.

Gwen reached across the table and rested her hand on his left forearm. His muscles were rigid beneath his soft sweater. "My children were very young when my husband and I divorced. Being a single parent under any circumstance is challenging. I can't imagine how hard it must have been, helping your children through their grief while you were coping with your own."

Noah looked away. "It was a difficult time."

Gwen waited for Noah to say more. He didn't elaborate, and she didn't push. "Did you have anyone to help you care for them?"

"I worked with a service to find a mature woman to take care of my sons after school and when I had to attend work events. But on James's sixteenth birthday, he told me he was done with 'babysitters.'" Noah's smile was tight and fleeting.

"The important thing is that you and your children worked through it."

"Sometimes I think we're still working through it."

Gwen sat back. There were ghosts in Noah's eyes. What wasn't he telling her? And what would it take to convince him to trust her?

****

"You want me to do another interview with *The Daily*?" Gwen gave Noah a skeptical look. "I'm still traumatized from our first interview with them."

Gwen and Noah were meeting in one of the Metropolitan Public Library's community rooms late Saturday afternoon.

They'd just finished a full day of debate practice. Before Noah had arrived, Gwen had arranged the room to simulate a debate setting. Two podiums stood in front of two groups of four short rows of empty chairs. Noah had assumed the role of Senator Dexter Jackson. After three days of debate preparation, Gwen was still trying to find her authentic voice.

The debate practices awoke vivid memories of their past relationship. She and Noah had had vigorous disagreements on many social issues: gun safety, criminal justice, education funding.

When had those healthy debates turned sour?

When she'd realized that they'd never find common ground.

Gwen had led Noah to the audience seats for a brief break and to review the list of Gwen's upcoming events, both scheduled and yet-to-be scheduled.

Noah tossed her a glance from his seat across the aisle. "This time, the interview will go well."

"Are they sending a different reporter?" Gwen took a swig from her bottle of water to wash down her sarcasm and ease her dry throat. Noah's confidence was like an aphrodisiac. There, she'd said it.

"It'll be Trevor again-"

Gwen interrupted with a groan of disgust.

Noah continued. "But we've been getting a lot of positive press from his competitors. As the community's oldest paper – not to mention the largest and most respected – Trevor's bosses will want to assume the lead on coverage of our campaign."

"All right. I'll be ready." Gwen struggled to keep her gaze on Noah's eyes and not his body.

"I know." Noah's lips curved in a half smile before he shifted his gaze to his Smart tablet. "You also have a meeting with several professional organizations, including the teachers association, medical association, firefighters union and police union."

Gwen's pulse thumped once with each group Noah read off. Nerves. She leaned back against the grape cushioned honey wood chair. "Your team has been busy."

"*Our* team, and yes they have." Noah slipped his tablet back into his briefcase before standing. He was tall and fit in a chocolate knit crewneck sweater, black khakis and black loafers. He inclined his head toward the podiums. "Are you ready to get back to it?"

"Of course." Gwen moved toward her podium on the right.

Almost two hours later, Noah wrapped up their practice session. Gwen led him back to the audience chairs. "Do you have an update on the debate schedule?"

"Dexter suggested a weekday afternoon."

"Why would he want to have a campaign debate when most people are at work?" The minute she asked the question, Gwen had the answer. "He's trying to suppress the viewing audience."

"Dexter doesn't want you to gain name recognition. He also doesn't want you to make him look bad."

"Senator Jackson has everything in his favor." Gwen allowed her anxiety to show. "His approval ratings are in the high forties. The state's unemployment rate is below the national average, and our economy is stable."

Noah counted off his fingers. "Dexter hasn't held any town hall meetings, hasn't sponsored meaningful legislation, and hasn't visited any communities in his district."

Gwen frowned. "What convinced you to be his campaign manager?"

Noah was silent as though considering his answer. "I thought the status quo was working. My business is turning a profit. My sons are gainfully employed. But our policies have to be about more than just *my* family. I read that on your group's website."

He'd read their website. Gwen hadn't expected that. "Our community is only as strong and as safe as our neighbors. Our families are successful now, but we aren't immune to the conditions around us, and those conditions *must* change."

Names and images scrolled across her mind like the black-and-white opening credits of a historical documentary. Rekia Boyd, 22, Chicago, March 21, 2012, just three days ago, killed by an off-duty police detective. Shereese Francis, 29, Queens, New York, March 15, 2012, suffocated as officers tried to handcuff her. Ramarley Graham, 18, Bronx, New York, Feb. 2, 2012, shot by police who'd entered his apartment without a warrant. And there were more names. Would there always be more names? When would it end?

Noah continued. "You woke me when you voiced your frustration with Dexter's avoiding your meetings. Trayvon Martin's murder increased the urgency."

"You're giving me too much credit." Gwen turned away to collect her tote bag and to avoid the look of admiration in Noah's eyes. It was giving her feelings.

"No, I'm not." Noah set his hand on Gwen's shoulder. She felt it all the way to her toes. "I was attracted to your passion the first time we met, but I didn't appreciate it. I was blinded by my own ambition back then. Now I realize that politics isn't a game."

Gwen's lips curved into a smile. "Well, better late than never."

Noah's gaze shifted from Gwen's eyes to her mouth. His hand tightened on her shoulder. He took a small step toward her, decimating the space between them. She could feel his warmth, smell his soap-and-mint scent.

His gaze returned to hers. There was a question in his eyes. Gwen swayed toward him in answer. Her gaze dropped to his full, moist lips. She'd been curious about their taste. Would her tongue remember it? She had to know. She needed to know. Now.

Gwen drifted toward Noah. He reached out as though to steady her. His hands were big and hot through the sleeves of her oversized sweater. Gwen lifted onto her toes, closer to Noah's mouth. A smart man, Noah took her cue and lowered his head to hers. Gwen parted her lips as Noah's mouth covered hers.

Gwen gasped. Noah's taste was intoxicating. Warm. Exciting. Heady. With his trademark confidence, he swept his tongue into her mouth. Gwen trembled in reaction. Noah tucked her closer against his body. Gwen melted against him. Through his sweater, she felt Noah's chest, crushing her breasts. His muscled arms held her against his hard torso. His tongue stroked against hers, teasing and tempting her to explore him. Gwen engaged him, suckling Noah's tongue deeper into her mouth. She heard his groan and answered with her own.

Noah's hips pressed against her. Gwen felt warm and restless. Too warm. Too restless. Her pulse drummed in her ears. She couldn't catch her breath. She stepped back and, after a beat, Noah dropped his arms.

Gwen swallowed. Her gaze remained glued to Noah's. "Oh, boy."

Noah looked as stunned as she felt. "That's an understatement." His rich, smooth baritone was like a drug to her already intoxicated senses.

Gwen locked her knees to keep from collapsing. "Now that our curiosity has been satisfied, we can concentrate on the campaign."

"Curiosity? Do you think that's all this is?"

Gwen cleared her throat. "That's all this can be, Noah. There's too much at stake for us to get romantically involved."

She shrugged into her coat, walking carefully out of the community room. Gwen was grateful that Noah remained behind, giving her space and time to recover. With echoes of desire still coursing through her, Gwen may have proven the lie about their attraction being only curiosity. But there was still too much at stake.

Chapter 8

"What are you doing here?" Gwen gripped the doorknob to keep from slamming her front door in her ex-husband's face Saturday night.

"Is that any way to speak to the father of your children?" William Gaston posed on Gwen's front steps, tall and slim in an expensive black cashmere coat.

Gwen restrained from rolling her eyes. Barely. "Drew and Maggie aren't here. I don't have to be civil to you."

"We've been divorced for almost twenty years, Gwen." William looked at her with pity. "When are you going to get over it? I have."

"I've noticed. Was it your second or third wife who bought you that coat?" Gwen saw the flash of anger in William's eyes before he masked it.

"I'm not here to argue with you, Gwen, although I know how much you enjoy it-"

"Not really."

William ignored her interruption. "I'm here to talk about our children. May I come in?"

"What about Drew and Maggie?" Gwen had spoken with her children yesterday. She told herself there was no cause for concern. Chances were William was simply playing on the only weaknesses he knew she had.

William shook his head. "I don't want to have this conversation on the front doorsteps. Invite me in."

Gwen stepped back albeit reluctantly. Humoring William was the only way to get rid of him. "Don't take off your coat. You're not staying."

William crossed her threshold as though he was walking onto a stage. The strength of his cologne almost choked her.

"Did you get new furniture?" William looked around the room.

Gwen could tell from his tone that he was estimating the value of every item in her foyer. "You're not here for an interior design update. Say what you came to say, then leave."

She couldn't stand to be in the same room with her ex-husband. Drew and Maggie were the only reasons she acknowledged his existence. Without him she wouldn't have her beautiful children, and she couldn't imagine her life without them.

William turned to face Gwen, rolling back and forth on the balls of his feet. "I saw the article about you in *The Daily*. You should've come to me to talk about running for state senate first before you announced your candidacy."

Gwen's temper stirred. She had enough practice dealing with William to know how to control it. "Why would I have to discuss my plans with you first?"

William's eyes widened, but Gwen couldn't tell whether his surprise was authentic. "I'm the father of your children. Whatever you do affects me."

"You're my ex-husband. Nothing I do affects you."

"The media will want to interview me about your campaign. They're going to want my perspective on your campaign and what kind of senator you'd make, if elected."

Gwen shrugged. "If the media contacts you, you can decline to speak with them. You're not obligated to grant them an interview."

"I'd think it would be my civic duty to give the press an interview."

"Your civic duty?" Gwen laughed. William's claim was too absurd to be taken seriously. "Since when do you care?"

"You don't want me to speak to reporters, do you?" William turned to face Gwen. His expression was sly.

Gwen realized William's intent with his surprise visit. "It's your decision, Bill."

"What if I decide to go ahead and do it? Is there anything you don't want me to tell the reporters?"

"I'm not worried about you talking to the media."

"Are you sure?"

"Positive. I don't have anything to hide. Although an argument could be made that our marriage is an example of bad judgment on my part." Gwen shrugged. "I don't completely agree with that, though, considering Drew and Maggie. But either way, our divorce redeems me."

William didn't look amused. "What about your parents' judgment? Some people would say they showed bad judgment by sneaking into the country."

They both knew her parents hadn't snuck into the United States. Their visas had expired. William was trying to bait her. Gwen refused to let him. "I'm not concerned about you discussing my parents with reporters."

Especially since Noah was well aware of the details of her parents' path to citizenship. Gwen was confident that he had a plan for navigating those details with the media, if that became necessary.

"Maybe you should be worried." William spread his arms. "For a financial consideration, I can promise you that the media will never find out about your parents' illegal status from me."

Gwen was almost speechless. Almost. "This is a new low, even for you, Bill." She crossed to her front door and jerked it open. "Leave. Now."

William crossed to her. "At least consider my offer. I can help you, Gwen. Or I can hurt you."

She unclenched her teeth. "I'll take my chances with the media."

Gwen exercised great restraint in not slamming the door behind William. It occurred to her that she wouldn't have felt as confident taking her chances with the media if Noah wasn't also on her side.

***

Late Sunday afternoon, Noah rang the doorbell of his eldest son's apartment. The thought had crossed his mind more than once that forcing another confrontation with James wasn't a great idea, especially since he was still reeling from kissing Gwen yesterday. That kiss had laid him out like a hit from a National Football League defensive lineman. Simple curiosity? He called bullshit.

Despite the turmoil in his mind and the lingering restlessness in his body, one thing was clear: No matter what was happening in his life, he couldn't – wouldn't – stop asking for his son's forgiveness. Although his brain had counseled him against getting into his car, Noah had found himself pulling into a parking space in the underground garage of James's apartment building.

James opened the door and pinned Noah with an expression of concern. "Is Clark OK?"

It concerned Noah that James was always so worried about his younger brother's welfare. Did James's anxiety stem from residual guilt?

"Clark's fine. I spoke with him earlier." Noah felt the waves of relief rolling off of his son. He took in James's alma mater's yellow-and-blue sweatshirt. It was his alma mater as well, and he was proud that both of his sons had attended it.

The scents of seasoned meat, spicy mustard, and savory stew drifted through the doorway. James must have just finished a lunch of hamburgers and soup. Had he eaten alone? He didn't know much about his son's life, personally or professionally.

James rubbed a hand over his face. "Unless something's wrong with Clark, don't come to my home uninvited again."

His firstborn stepped back and started to close the door in Noah's face. Noah's right arm shot up to prevent James from shutting him out.

"Son, I just want to talk." His voice was firm but gentle just as it had been when he'd explained to a four-year-old James why he couldn't draw on the living room wall with his new finger paints.

James's lips tightened. "Talk, then, but don't call me that."

Noah lowered his arm. "May I come in?"

"No." James displayed a familiar contempt that was slowly killing Noah.

Noah ignored the pain in his chest and forged forward. "I take full responsibility for everything that happened almost ten years ago. Everything. What do I have to do for you to accept my apology?"

James's lips twisted with bitterness. "Turn back time."

Noah swallowed, forcing back the lump in his throat. "I wish I could, son. I wish I could have found some way to do just that."

Some way to go back in time to prevent that gunman from killing all of those people in Wedgewood Baptist Church. Some way to prevent that gunman from even entering the church. Some way to keep that gunman from getting a gun.

Some way to save the mother of his sons.

James's squared jaw hardened like granite. "Is that what you've been looking for in all of those bottles of Jack Daniels? A time machine?"

Noah sucked in a breath. How many more body blows could he take? As many as he needed to until he'd earned his son's forgiveness. "I've been dry since that night."

Since that night James had called child protective services hoping to find someone who could better take care of his younger brother. Noah didn't know how he'd managed to talk his way out of that one. It had been the most sobering experience of his life. A reality check with a vengeance, but his son had saved his life.

"And you have what, sixteen days to go? Do you think you'll make it?" James's grunt of acknowledgement was dismissive.

Another two weeks and two days until April eighth, the night he'd stopped drinking. He wasn't surprised James remembered the date as clearly as he did.

"I do." Noah raised his chin, struggling against the weight of his shame. "Will you forgive me then?"

"I doubt it."

"Then what can I do to help you forgive yourself?"

James stepped back, giving Noah a furious look. This time, Noah let the door slam in his face. He turned to slowly walk out of the apartment building and back to his car.

Ten years ago, he wished he'd found some way to protect

his son from having to make the most difficult decision of his young life. If he'd accepted responsibility then, James wouldn't be punishing them both now.

***

"I can tell something's bothering you." Edwina gave Gwen a searching look as they left the breakroom after lunch on this final Monday in March. Her eyes were dark with concern. "What's on your mind?"

"Noah kissed me on Saturday. And I kissed him back." Gwen hadn't meant to blurt that information so indelicately, but there it was.

Edwina grabbed Gwen's wrist and led her back to her office. She closed the door before freeing Gwen. "Tell me everything."

Her office had been comfortably warm this morning. Now it felt stifling. Gwen stepped back, giving her friend a grumpy look.

"This is serious. Yes, Noah's handsome, but he's also my campaign manager, which means he's off limits."

Edwina settled onto one of the visitor's chairs. She crossed her long legs in her scarlet pants suit and leaned forward. "Who initiated the kiss?"

"I would characterize it as a mutual initiation." Gwen winced at her defensive tone. She turned to take her seat behind her desk. The scent of dark coffee pinched her nose. Gwen glanced at her empty mug. She'd forgotten to wash it before leaving for lunch. That was out-of-character for her.

"Ah."

Gwen looked up at her friend. "What does that mean?"

"It's obvious. If the initiation was mutual, then the attraction must be mutual as well."

"That's not surprising." Restless, Gwen stood again to pace her cozy office. "The attraction was definitely mutual last time, too."

"But this time, in addition to the physical attraction, you've also had a meeting of the minds. What are you going to do about it?"

Gwen turned to pace back toward the window beside her desk. "I'm going to ignore it."

"Why?" Edwina's voice lifted with surprise.

"There's too much at stake to risk the election by having a personal relationship with Noah." Gwen paced back toward her closed office door. "We couldn't get *The Daily* reporter to focus on my campaign message the first time we met with him. All he was interested in was Noah's leaving Dexter's campaign. Could you imagine what it would be like if there were rumors of our having an affair? We'd never get the media to talk about anything else."

"What a waste." Edwina stood. "If you ask me, those are two separate things: a relationship with your attractive campaign manager and, separately, your policy proposals."

"I can't risk it."

"I think it's worth the risk," Edwina sang over her shoulder as she left Gwen's office.

As if on cue, her desk phone rang. Gwen answered it on reflex. "Metropolitan Public Library. Gwen Taylor speaking. How may I help you?"

"Good afternoon, Ms. Taylor. This is Ned Dennison. I'm Senator Jackson's aide, actually, I'm calling to help you." The voice was young, perhaps a college intern or recent graduate.

Gwen's intuition put her on high alert. "Help me in what way?"

"I'm going to offer you some good advice. Pull out of the campaign now."

"That sounds more like a threat than advice." Gwen kept her voice cool despite the temper straining to pick up steam.

"Senator Jackson is the candidate the party has chosen to represent us in the twenty-twelve election. There's no point in your wasting your time or money going against him. Maybe next time." The condescension dripping from his tongue further rankled Gwen.

She imagined some baby-faced young man sitting in a common office area with a dozen other underpaid, overworked, clueless interns with delusions of grandeur. Or worse; he could be sitting in a private office bestowed on him by cronyism, afforded little guidance by possible role models and given even far less understanding of his responsibilities.

"If Senator Jackson is representing the party, who's representing the people?"

Boy Wonderless chuckled. "Senator Jackson will, of course."

Gwen tightened her grip on both her beige telephone receiver and her temper. "This isn't about parties. This is about serious issues affecting real people, issues that Senator Jackson continues to ignore."

"What issues?" Ned didn't seem aware his asking that question was a confession of his lack of interest.

"It boils down to racism, Ned."

His laughter interrupted her. "America's just elected a black president. Racism is dead."

Gwen tasted the bile rising in her throat. "The fact that you can say that – and mean it – proves that no one in your campaign is qualified to represent this community. Read a newspaper. Racism doesn't affect only black, brown, Asian and Native Americans. It's a danger to the country as a whole."

"What makes you think you have more qualifications for office than an incumbent senator? You're a librarian." Ned said that like it was a bad thing.

"Obviously, you've never been to a library, Ned. Why don't you stop by and I'll give you a tour of this one."

"You'll have trouble raising the money you'll need for the campaign." Ned had taken off his gloves. The spite in his voice came through loudly and clearly – and childishly. It gave insight into the kind of people working on Dexter's campaign. "Do you think you can outraise the Senator? You can't."

If Ned had decided to drop reasoning in favor of scaring her, it would have worked – if Gwen hadn't been so angry. "All the money in the world won't help your candidate if you don't have a platform to promote or achievements to point to."

"The Senator's not going to go easy on you just because you're a political novice."

"I won't go easy on him, either."

Ned sounded like he was gnashing his teeth. "You only have two months to build your name. That kind of thing takes money – a lot of it. You don't have time to raise that kind of cash."

"Watch me." Gwen disconnected the call.

She sat at her desk with her hand lingering on the receiver, waiting for her breathing to calm and her pulse to slow. She could have handled the call better. On the bright side, maybe this call was a good sign for her campaign. Dexter must feel threatened by her. Why else would he have had his aide try to intimidate her?

***

So this was Gwen's ex-husband.

Noah sat across the table in the small conference room, studying the other man Monday afternoon. Curiosity rather than courtesy had prompted Noah to accept William Gaston's unscheduled visit when the other man had announced his presence in their office suite.

He supposed women would consider William good-looking. Touches of gray hid among the thick brown curls that framed his fair face. He was tall – about Noah's height – and slim in a dark silver Italian designer suit. Judging by the suit and Italian shoes, Gwen's ex was doing well for himself. But there was something in his toothy grin that branded him untrustworthy.

"I'll make this quick since we're both busy men." William flashed more teeth. He was a dentist's dream.

"I appreciate that." Noah's irony seemed lost on his uninvited guest.

William had settled back onto the black cloth conference chair as though he owned the suite and the building it was in. His hands, now linked across his slightly protruding abdomen, had been soft to the touch when Noah had greeted him.

"Of course." William waved his manicured hand in a dismissive gesture. "I read in The Daily that you're managing my ex-wife's campaign. I'll continue to keep silent about certain negative information I have on Gwen in return for a financial consideration. This is the same offer I made to Gwen."

The same offer I made to Gwen.

Noah's mouth went dry. His tongue tasted like dust. When had William made the offer and why hadn't Gwen told him about her ex-husband's attempt at blackmail? As her campaign manager, Noah was disappointed on a professional level. As an old friend, he was hurt on a personal level.

He set those feelings aside and prepared to Bogart his way through this impromptu meeting. "What makes you think my reaction would be any different from Gwen's?"

William gave Noah a sly smile as he swung his chair from side-to-side. "You have more experience in this arena. You know how the game is played."

Noah could see why Gwen had divorced William. Once their campaign was over and Gwen was seated in the senate, Noah would ask her why she'd married the other man in the first place.

He balanced his right ankle on his left knee, and prepared to go fishing. "What sort of negative information do you have on her?"

Noah was confident that Foster Capehart, the investigator he'd been hiring for years to perform his candidates' background checks, hadn't missed even a comma during his research. But William's response to this question would tell Noah a lot. Would Gwen's ex-husband go so far as to lie? And to whom would he be willing to feed false information, the media? Dexter?

William shrugged with apparent nonchalance. "Gwen and I were married for many years. A long time. I have all sorts of dirt on her."

"Such as?"

"For the right price, not only will I withhold the negative stuff, but I'll personally go to the media and sing Gwen's praises." William straightened on his chair and spread his arms. "If not, I'll make things harder for her to be elected. You see, Noah – can I call you Noah?" When Noah remained silent, William continued. "I can be your campaign's best friend or its worst enemy. It's your choice."

"You still haven't told me what kind of information you have."

William tried a taunting smile. "I don't want to play my hand."

Noah smelled the first faint traces of desperation wafting from William. "I think it's more likely that you don't have any negative information." He set both feet on the ground and leaned into the glass conference table toward William. "You and Gwen have been divorced longer than you were married. Your marriage was less than nine years old before she divorced you for adultery."

Surprise froze William's pretty features but the other man made an effort to rally. "I do have dirt on Gwen."

"No, you don't." Noah gave William a hard, direct stare. "But we have dirt on you."

William's glare was furious. "Gwen may be clean, but her parents weren't."

"You don't have the right to smear Gwen's dead parents, especially when you have so many secrets that you'd like to keep hidden." Noah had practically memorized Foster's notes on William Gaston. "This isn't your first extortion attempt, is it? Your current wife – your third, right? – is very wealthy. Was that part of her appeal? Does she know you have an arrest record that includes charges for check forgeries? Does she know about your arrest for embezzlement or that you still haven't mastered the fidelity part of your wedding vows?"

Shock drained some of the color from William's face. "How do you know about that? How do you know any of this?"

Sensing he'd made his point, Noah sat back. "If you continue to threaten Gwen and our campaign, if you hurt Gwen in any way, I'll provide the information I have on you to your very wealthy wife. You see, William, I can be your best friend or your worst enemy. It's your choice."

William gave Noah a parting glare before springing from his chair and storming from the conference room. Through the glass-and-wood-paned doors, Noah watched Gwen's ex-husband march past Sandy, his administrative assistant, and out of the suite. He didn't know if he'd be able to wait until after Gwen was sworn into the state senate to ask why she'd married William. His curiosity was just too strong.

Noah stood to return to his office. He'd have to tell Gwen about his encounter with her ex-husband – and ask why she'd withheld information about her meeting with him. Secrets between them could jeopardize their campaign. Neither of them could afford to be blindsided again.

CHAPTER 9

Blood pounded in Gwen's ears. The air in the police department's meeting room was thick with hostility Monday evening. Glares from members of the local Unity of Police Cooperative who'd attended her campaign presentation bore into her. The cooperative was a local chapter of a national association that worked to advance the interests of police officers through legislation and political involvement. She could smell their antagonism. Gwen locked her knees and strove to appear unfazed.

She tossed a look toward the back of the room where *The Daily* reporter sat. Trevor Hollis seemed bored. He'd taken a few notes during Gwen's speech in what was probably an effort to stay awake.

"That concludes my presentation. Thank you for your time and attention. I'm happy to answer your questions." It was obvious that something was weighing on their minds.

"Why do you want to repeal the Second Amendment?" A burly blond with angry blue eyes shot the question at her from the front row.

Gwen was certain repealing the Second Amendment wasn't on her platform much less in her speech. Had the angry man heard a word she'd said? She glanced at the questioner's two-stripe insignia on the arm of his uniform jacket. "May I ask your name, Corporal?"

Some of his antagonism drained, leaving only confusion. "Appleby."

Gwen's attention was drawn to Trevor. He'd started taking notes again. Stifling a sigh, Gwen returned to the corporal. "Corporal Appleby, why do you think I want to take away the right that citizens of the United States have to bear arms?"

A George Clooney look alike seated at the back of the room spoke up. "The senator's aide, Ned Dennison, said that you're anti-law enforcement and anti-Second Amendment."

Gwen struggled with dismay over the actions Dexter and his team had taken to undermine her to local associations before she could introduce herself. Of even greater concern was the fact that the cooperative's members had accepted Dexter's lies as truth without giving her a chance.

She sensed Noah standing behind her. He'd warned her that Dexter had committed to a fully negative campaign. She'd better strap in and get ready for it.

Gwen stepped away from the podium. She crossed into the aisle between the two groupings of brown metal folding chairs. Her eyes dipped to the three-stripe sergeant insignia on the arm of the uniform jacket belonging to the George Clooney doppelganger. "What's your name, Sergeant?"

"Bates." His resentment was palpable.

Gwen focused on Sergeant Bates. She tried to ignore Trevor who sat a few rows in front of the sergeant, recording their exchange with newfound enthusiasm.

"Sergeant Bates, it sounds as though Senator Jackson led you to believe that I'd have the power to disappear the Second Amendment with a stroke of my pen. Senator Jackson is mistaken.

And it should concern all of us that he's so unfamiliar with the Constitution."

Sergeant Bates crossed his arms. "He said you'd push for it."

"He makes it sound easy, but amending the Constitution is actually a very long and complicated process." Gwen counted off on her fingers the procedural steps. "Amendments require approval by a super majority in both houses of Congress and the states, as well as a presidential signature."

"But you'd bring us one step closer to its being repealed," Corporal Appleby asserted.

Gwen shifted to face him. "No, I wouldn't. Dexter Jackson is not a member of my campaign. He doesn't speak for me. In fact, Senator Jackson has proven time and again that the only person he represents is himself."

Corporal Appleby shifted on his seat to confront her. "So you're not a member of that neighborhood policing group?"

Gwen held Corporal Appleby's gaze. "I'm not just a member. I'm a cofounder."

Corporal Appleby's eyes hardened. "Your organization undermines the city's police force."

"You're mistaken." Gwen returned to the front of the room. "I'm not anti-law enforcement. I'm anti-abuse of power. I'm anti-innocent, unarmed people being killed by vigilantes and rogue police officers."

The room erupted. Members of the city's police department were shouting questions at her and demanding answers all at once. Gwen heard one question raised above the others.

"How do you know those officers weren't just trying to protect themselves?"

Gwen turned to her accuser, a thin young man of average height. Some of his acne scars were as red as his hair. "The F.B.I.

has been tracking killings by police since 2000. Its data is based on information voluntarily collected from members of police forces across the country. This information shows that the numbers of so-called justifiable homicides are increasing each year. Is that a trend we should live with?"

"Can you live with the crime on the streets?" The thin corporal shouted.

Gwen counselled herself to keep calm. "Thank you for your question. Also according to the F.B.I., violent crime rates dropped substantially in the nineteen-nineties even as the number of so-called justifiable homicides by police is increasing. Why aren't the police killings also dropping?" Gwen gazed around the room. "We need an answer to that question." The room remained silent. "If our officers are afraid, then police departments need better employment screenings and better training. Do you want to go on patrols with someone who's that afraid? Wouldn't he or she be a greater danger to you than an unarmed individual? My goal is to protect *you* as well as the community *you* promised to protect."

Gwen paused again, waiting for their response. It came in the form of a tense silence and angry stares. Trevor was the only one in the room who seemed happy to be there.

Gwen gathered her notes. "Again, thank you for your time. I hope you'll consider my message."

She looked over her shoulder as Noah joined her. Leaving the community room in a sea of silence, Gwen felt like they were walking the gauntlet. At least she wasn't alone.

"That could have gone better," she whispered.

"It could have gone worse," Noah muttered back.

They found Noah's Honda in the parking lot and settled into the car. Gwen was glad she'd allowed Noah to persuade her to carpool with him. She was too agitated and tense to drive, and anyway the awkwardness between them after Saturday's kiss was long forgotten.

Gwen clenched the purse that sat on her lap. "I shouldn't be surprised that Senator Jackson's campaign is distorting my message. That's what politicians do to their opponents."

"Not all politicians, but Dexter is a master of the negative craft." Noah pulled out of the parking space and guided his sedan toward the lot's exit. "Maybe you should ease up on the rhetoric on police shootings."

"I won't do that, Noah." Gwen stared through the windshield. "I'm right, and I'm not going to change my position just to get votes or because it's the easier path to take. This is about what my community needs, not about what's politically expedient or comfortable. And one of the many things my community needs is to be safe."

"I understand that, but you're alienating a lot of voters with this message and it's not only police officers."

The passion Gwen felt on this subject poured out of her. "Gun fanatics think their Second Amendment rights supersede my right and my neighbors' right to feel safe in our communities. They don't."

Noah slowed his car and checked his mirrors. "It's that kind of messaging that makes gun owners question your intent with the Second Amendment. Not all gun owners are fanatics."

"Gun violence is gun violence, whether that gun belongs to some vigilante like George Zimmerman or to a police officer."

"Gwen, all I'm suggesting is that you dial down the rhetoric just a little so you don't scare away votes."

"If my position won't earn my neighbors' votes, then so be it. I'll accept that I'm not the person to represent them." She stared through the windshield, realizing that Noah had pulled into another space in the parking lot. He apparently didn't want to drive while arguing. She could respect that.

"Those are good points-"

"It's more than police shooting black people without punishment, as horrible as that is. It's the higher unemployment rates, the disparity in housing, in business loans, in school punishments, in health care. The list goes on, Noah. We must enforce – and in many cases – enact new policies or strengthen existing policies that combat these disparities."

"Is that all?" Noah spoke quietly.

"Yes."

"You're right. I agree with everything you've said. We'll do it your way. We'll let your message drive the campaign."

Gwen eased her grip on her purse. "Thank you."

"No, thank *you*." Noah caught her eyes. "You're making me want to be a positive force in the community instead of a spectator profiting from the game. If you can have that effect on me, you can have that effect on others."

Gwen felt flustered. "You make me feel as though I can do anything."

"I believe that you can." Noah once again maneuvered his Honda out of a parking space and toward the lot's exit. "Now that we've resolved that matter, we can move on to the next item on this evening's agenda."

"What's that?" Gwen forced herself to relax back onto the cream cloth passenger seat. She took a deep breath and drew in Noah's now familiar soap-and-mint scent. She wasn't cold anymore.

"William Gaston came to speak with me this afternoon." Noah merged his Honda into traffic, then stopped at a red light.

"Bill?" Gwen's eyes widened on Noah's chiseled profile. "What did he want?"

Noah briefly took his attention from the traffic signal. "He wanted to be paid to keep negative stories about you out of the media. He said he'd made the same offer to you."

Hindsight was twenty-twenty. "It was a similar offer. I should have told you about that. I'm sorry."

"We can't keep secrets from each other." The traffic signal turned green. Noah moved his car forward. "The campaign would've been blindsided if he'd gone to the media."

"Bill wouldn't have gone to the media. He knows they wouldn't be interested in his information."

"But he could've gone to Dexter, who would've been more than happy to distort the truth."

"Oh."

"Yes."

It was almost eight o'clock in the evening, but it wasn't dark yet. The days were longer since they'd observed daylight savings more than two weeks ago on March eleventh.

Gwen stared through the passenger window. Instead of seeing the other cars on the freeway, and the hospitals, restaurants and buildings in the nearby neighborhoods, she recollected images from her last confrontation with William. Her ex-husband had always been more trouble than he was worth.

"You're right. I thought I'd handled the situation." The words were out before Gwen realized she would say them.

"You don't have to handle these situations alone. We're a team. We have to handle them together."

Together. Gwen liked the sound of that. She'd felt alone for far too long. Although Noah was referring to the campaign, a growing part of Gwen wished he was talking about something more. But was that desire worth the risk to their campaign?

***

"Is it true that the two of you are having a personal relationship?" Trevor waited as though he expected an answer to his inappropriate question.

Gwen wouldn't have thought anything could have gone worse than her presentation to the local Unity of Police Cooperative two days earlier. But as she sat in Noah's small conference room with him and the reporter from hell, she acknowledged that she was wrong. This interview was worse than her presentation to the angry police officers. Way worse.

Noah must feel the same way. He went tense beside her. "My relationships with my clients are always professional and unassailable."

That wasn't strictly true, but this wasn't the time to bring up their kiss on that Saturday afternoon four days ago. Gwen's body warmed thinking about it. She forced away those images, tastes and touches, and instead made herself focus on Trevor's questions.

"What makes you think that Noah and I are in a personal relationship?"

Trevor shifted his attention from Noah to Gwen. "Ned Dennison implied that you two were dating."

Gwen counted to ten. "Mr. Dennison is Senator Jackson's aide. He doesn't work with our campaign. He doesn't speak for us. Don't allow him to feed you innuendoes and lies."

Trevor split a dubious look from Noah to Gwen. "It's all right if you are. You're both consenting, single adults. I could understand if you choose to have a clandestine relationship."

"That's magnanimous of you." Gwen bit back an angrier retort.

"You're welcome." Trevor eyed her with suspicion, seeming to sense but not quite certain of her sarcasm.

"Let's get to more important campaign issues, like our policy positions." Noah jumped into the exchange as though trying to rescue a swimmer who was sinking for a second time.

Trevor turned to Gwen. "The members of the police cooperative were pretty hard on you yesterday. Did your experience during your presentation make you rethink your position on law enforcement?"

Gwen saw the trap the reporter had prepared. "Let me be clear. I'm very supportive of law enforcement. I always will be. This is a safety issue, a life-and-death issue that our country doesn't have the luxury of walking away from. For the safety of civilians – and police officers – law enforcement agencies must screen out officers who are ill-equipped for this dangerous job and those who go into it for the wrong reasons."

The rest of the interview was more productive if still somewhat tense. Gwen didn't relax until after Noah returned from escorting Trevor out of the office suite.

He tossed her a victory grin as he reclaimed his seat beside her. "This interview went a lot better than the first one."

"I wouldn't go that far." Gwen's voice was tight. "Dexter has crossed the line with this latest dirty campaign trick. Planting lies that we're having an affair is going way too far. We have to stop him."

Noah shook his head. "We're better off ignoring him and the rumors. His goal is to pull us off message. He doesn't want to campaign on policy because he knows he'll lose."

Gwen wasn't buying it. "Dexter Jackson reminds me of a dog that pees on your carpet. If you ignore his bad behavior, he'll just keep doing it."

"But if you address every inconsequential comment Dexter makes, he'll distract us from our goal, which is taking his seat."

"Inconsequential? How can you consider rumors about our having an affair inconsequential to our campaign?"

"Because we aren't having an affair. Are we?"

Heat exploded inside Gwen, strumming against the muscles of her lower abdomen. He had to ask her that? "I'm pretty certain that if we were sleeping together, at least one of us would be aware of it."

Noah spun his chair and pulled it farther under the glass table. "My advice is to channel that fighting spirit into the campaign. You'll be a lot more productive."

Gwen rose from her seat. She adjusted her purse on her shoulder as she prepared to leave. "I'll take your advice. For now."

Noah stood beside her. "I'll pick you up from your house Friday night so we can drive together to the fund-raiser Cynthia and Kenneth are hosting."

Gwen led the way to the conference room door. "I'm still nervous about the event. I've asked people to donate to the library but I've never asked them to give *me* money. Do you have any other suggestions on how I should conduct myself?"

Noah reached around her to open the door. Gwen caught his scent. For a moment, she was tempted to lean into his warmth.

What was wrong with her? They weren't idealistic twenty-somethings anymore. They were pragmatic fifty-somethings, well aware of the potential consequences of their actions. She hurried through the door, forcing stray images of Noah's arms from her mind.

Noah kept pace beside her. "You don't have any reason to be nervous. Just-"

"Stay on message."

Noah turned to retrieve Gwen's coat. He helped her into it before shrugging into his own. "Exactly. And I'll be right beside you the entire night."

On that note, Noah escorted Gwen to her car. She wondered whether she'd be able to sleep tonight without thoughts of Noah invading her dreams.

***

Friday evening, Gwen walked away from the podium on trembling legs. She'd just welcomed a ballroom full of expensively dressed guests to her fund-raiser in the city's swankiest hotel – all courtesy of Cynthia and Kenneth. The room reeked of money.

As director of the Metropolitan Library System, Gwen was used to asking donors for money for the library. Public speaking had always terrified her, though. She wasn't a fan of putting herself in front of a swarm of people. But if that's what it took to get the state senate seat, she was all in.

"Well done." Kenneth shook her hand as she stepped off the makeshift stage. He was tall and handsome in his black suit, chalk white shirt and emerald-and-white tie.

"You were awesome." Cynthia pulled Gwen into a tight, celebratory hug.

"Thank you." Gwen once again admired Cynthia's white-and-azure satin evening gown, and the pearl-and-sapphire jewels woven into the braids she'd arranged on the crown of her head.

Noah joined them. He pressed a flute of champagne into Gwen's hands, but he seemed to be drinking fruit punch. "You need to mingle while the message is still fresh in their minds."

After Kenneth's and Cynthia's encouragement, Noah's brusque instructions were somewhat deflating. She gave a mental shrug and considered the three-quarters-full champagne flute she'd accepted from Noah. She was tempted to toss back its contents, but that probably wasn't a good idea. In the short term, the champagne may settle her nerves, but in the long-term, the potential headlines would destroy her campaign.

"And I know just the couple to start with." Cynthia placed a gentle hand against Gwen's back to nudge her forward.

Two women stepped into their path. The more serious of the two pinned Gwen with a confrontational look. The other woman only had eyes for Noah.

"You're reckless." The serious one didn't waste time tossing down the gauntlet.

Cynthia sighed. "Florette, you and I have talked about this."

"Why do you think I'm being reckless?" Gwen took her challenger's measure. Florette's modest scoop-necked black cashmere dress screamed understated wealth. Glossy dark brown curls framed delicate, warm brown features.

"I see why she wanted to steal you away from Dexsy." The comment came from Florette's willowy companion who gazed up at Noah as though he was being served with the hors d'oeuvres. Her porcelain cheeks were flushed, and she must have paid a month of Gwen's salary to get her mass of strawberry blonde tresses so perfectly tousled.

"No one stole me from the senator." Noah's tone was firm. "I left his campaign."

"Markie, how many drinks have you had?" Cynthia placed herself between Noah and his new admirer.

Florette continued. "Our party has chosen our candidate. All you're doing with this primary is giving our opponents ammunition to smear the senator in their race against him."

Cynthia clamped a hand onto Markie's upper arm. "Markie, you are sexually harassing that man with your eyes. Stop it."

Gwen confronted Florette's condemnation. "My campaign isn't smearing Senator Jackson. I'm running on issues, specifically education funding, employment opportunities, gun safety and criminal justice reform. If Senator Jackson truly is our party's candidate, he should be willing and able to do the same."

Florette's voice shook with frustration. "Instead of campaigning against the senator, why don't you try talking to him?"

Gwen counted to ten and reconsidered her sarcasm. "I've tried that. The senator ignored me. How long must we wait for meetings that never occur while our children are taught with books that are more than ten years old in classrooms with mold growing up the walls? Minimum wage isn't keeping up with the cost of living. And neighbors are being murdered on our streets. I'm done with begging our public servants to serve. If he won't, then I must."

"You're wrong." Florette stepped closer. "You'll lose to the senator in the primary. Then, because of the damage you've done to his reputation with voters, the senator will lose to our opponent in the general election. You may think things are bad now. You have no idea. Watch what happens when the other side's in charge. And it will be all. Your. Fault." Florette grabbed Markie's arm. "We're leaving."

Startled, Markie waved an awkward salute to Noah. "Bye, handsome."

Gwen watched them leave. "Did they pay seven-hundred-and-fifty dollars each just to tell me to get out of the race?"

"It looks that way." Noah's voice was pensive.

Kenneth crossed his arms. "An email would've been free."

CHAPTER 10

"After that awful showing in the debate last night, it's not surprising that *The Daily* endorsed Dexter in the party's primary." Cynthia kicked off their post-debate evaluation meeting on a low note. Her expression was a study in disgust.

Gwen sat beside Noah at the oak table in the power couple's spacious dining room after work Wednesday evening. The aforementioned newspaper lay in the center of the dining room table. Gwen eyed it the same way she would a skunk that had sprayed her.

Her first political debate with Dexter had been held at a community college in front of an audience much larger than Gwen had anticipated. She'd frozen. Literally. Her vocal cords had tightened. Her mind had gone blank. The moderator had given Gwen the first question. She'd been unable to hear it above the sound of the blood draining from her head.

Nightmares of her poor performance had disrupted her sleep throughout the night. After the debate and well into the morning, one question had haunted her: *Have I made a mistake?*

Defeat weighed on Gwen like ankle chains. "My performance will hurt my poll numbers as well as the campaign's fund-raising. What can we do to recover from it?"

Cynthia turned her disgust to Noah. "Did you even prep her?"

"Not well enough." Noah straightened on his seat next to Gwen. He'd hung the jacket to his gunmetal gray suit and his navy tie on the back of his chair, and had rolled up the sleeves of his ice blue shirt. He looked tired – and sexy as heck.

Gwen raised both of her hands, palms out and faced Cynthia. As usual, her friend looked like royalty in a full-length jade cocoon dress accessorized with chunky silver jewelry. "I take full responsibility for this failure. No one else is to blame. I just froze. It won't happen again."

"We know." Kenneth cradled his coffee mug in his large hands as he looked around the table. "This was Gwen's first political debate. She didn't wipe the floor with Jackson, but she didn't run out of the building, either."

Gwen blinked. "That's the most I've ever heard you say at one time."

"Kenneth's right." Noah rubbed the back of his neck. "We can recover from a case of nerves. We couldn't have recovered from a televised meltdown."

"All right." Cynthia squeezed her husband's forearm. "Let's focus on the next debate. It's the last chance we'll have to give voters the opportunity to compare you to Dexter."

Nerves rattled in Gwen's abdomen like cubes of ice. If Cynthia's words were meant to reassure her, they failed decisively.

The next two hours flew past Gwen as she worked with Noah, Cynthia and Kenneth to prepare for the final debate. It was scheduled for the second week of May, three weeks before the primary election. High stakes indeed.

They also reviewed Gwen's schedule for the rest of April. It included fund-raisers and presentations to the teachers union, medical associations and community activist groups.

Gwen looked up to find Kenneth studying her.

"You're dead on your feet." Kenneth checked his silver Movado wristwatch.

"I hadn't realized it was so late." Cynthia stood. "We've done enough for tonight. Noah, take our candidate home so she can get some rest."

"We'll pick this up again this weekend." Noah rose and held Gwen's chair. He followed Kenneth and Cynthia, escorting Gwen to the front door.

"Don't dwell on the debate." Cynthia gave Gwen a quick, tight hug. "It's in the past. We need to start fresh for the next one."

Gwen struggled to give her friends a natural and confident smile. Hopefully, tomorrow she'd feel as optimistic as Cynthia sounded.

***

Gwen's sleepless night was catching up with her as Noah navigated his Honda away from the Anthonys' residence and toward Gwen's home. Her body felt like a wet noodle, but she couldn't shut off her mind.

Gwen rolled her head against the passenger seat's headrest and looked at Noah. "What made me think I'd be able to do this?"

"The fact that you can." Noah parked in front of her driveway. The streetlight in front of her house illuminated the right side of his face. The rest of his body was cast in shadow.

"I made a fool of myself last night." The words were hard, but there wasn't anyone else she'd rather be talking to about this.

"You showed your toughness." Noah gave her his half smile. "You were nervous, but you didn't give in to it. You stuck it out. That's what fighters do."

Gwen turned away from the admiration in his eyes. Through the windshield, she considered the ten wide steps that led from the sidewalk to her home's front door. It would be quite the climb tonight. "Obviously, I didn't fight hard enough. I cost our campaign the endorsement from *The Daily*."

"*The Daily* is a conservative paper. We were never going to get their backing."

Gwen only half heard him. The weeks upon weeks of long days spent preparing for last night's debate just to have it culminate in an epic failure had drained her mind, body and spirit. "I need to start thinking strategically, like a politician."

"No." Noah's sharp word startled her. "You're not running to be a politician. You're running to be an advocate in office."

He'd taken her breath away. "So you have been listening to me."

"I've always listened to you. I just haven't always heard you." His voice was rough with self-incriminations. "I finally understand what you tried to explain to me decades ago."

"There were so many things. Which specifically are you referring to?" Gwen watched Noah's sigh expand his chest beneath his still-crisp ice blue shirt.

Noah looked away, seeming to study the quiet, darkening street outside their intimate surroundings. "The basic rights our forefathers and foremothers marched, fought and died for aren't preserved in stone. We have to keep marching and fighting to protect them."

"We have to repay those who came before us for their sacrifices by protecting those rights for the generations who'll come after us." Gwen remembered saying those sentiments to him so many years ago.

"I get it now. Another sign that I'm evolving." Noah tossed her another smile.

Gwen considered Noah's face, part light, part shadow. "Your evolution is very sexy." The words were a whisper he wasn't supposed to hear.

But he had.

Noah's gaze – deep and dark – locked on hers. Gwen couldn't speak. She couldn't move. She could barely breathe. The heat in the car became as thick and itchy as a wool sweater. A sharp click shattered the heavy silence. Gwen dropped her gaze to Noah's hips. Slowly, his seatbelt shifted free, sliding across his lap. She looked again at his face and saw the question darkening his eyes. Gwen held her breath – and unhooked her seatbelt.

Noah shifted toward her. They met at the emergency brake. His muscled arms were firm around her waist. Beneath her palms, his chest was warm and hard; his heart beat was strong and steady. Gwen was mesmerized as Noah's head lowered to hers. Her eyes slipped shut, shrinking her world to touch, taste and scent.

His lips were firm and warm as they pressed against hers. Gwen opened her mouth, welcoming him. Noah's tongue traced her lips. He tasted of the coffee they'd had at the Anthonys' home. Gwen shivered at the hot, wet strokes against her skin. She parted her lips and Noah's tongue swept between them.

Suddenly, Gwen wasn't tired any longer.

Noah moved closer, holding her tighter. Gwen felt cherished. Desired. Safe. Every muscle in her body was alive and vibrating. She curled her fingers into his chest and gripped his shirt. The past and present crashed together. The memory of Noah's touch and taste and scent from decades earlier awakened feelings in her body today. Gwen wriggled closer to Noah, wanting to crawl onto the driver's seat and curl on top of him. She suckled his tongue, pulling it deeper into her mouth. Noah's moan was heat and hunger. Moisture pooled between Gwen's thighs.

Noah's lips drifted tiny kisses down her neck, generating an almost electric current under her skin. His hand slid up her side to cup her breast. His palm molded her, gently shaping her. His thumb caressed her breast's peak through her thin, knit sweater. Her nipple tightened, responding to his touch.

"Gwen." Noah's voice was rough. His breath was gentle against her ear.

Gwen's lips parted, waiting for him to return. She managed to respond with a sigh.

"Honey, let's go inside." He held her closer. The emergency brake pressed against her stomach.

Inside? Where ...?

Good Lord! She was making out in a car.

Gwen pushed away from Noah even as her body yearned toward him. Noah's hands fell away from her. Confusion mixed with desire in his eyes.

Gwen tried a calming breath. It didn't work.

"Noah. I'm so sorry. Carried away. We can't. Not now. People already suspect. We know the truth. Our messaging is at risk."

She was babbling. Her body was burning. Gwen sensed Noah's conflict. It echoed her own. But everything was at stake. Everything.

Noah sat back against his seat and scrubbed his hands over his face. "You're right." His voice was muffled against his palms. In the beats of silence, Gwen heard their breaths. Finally, Noah dropped his hands. "I'll walk you to your door."

Gwen didn't wait for him to open her door. She met Noah on the sidewalk. The night was cool, reducing the heat their bodies had generated in the car. Gwen preceded Noah up her front steps.

"Thank you again for driving." She fit her key into her front door lock.

Noah followed her across her front threshold. Gwen closed the door, then watched as he stood with his hands in his front pants pockets. From his vantage point, he could see through the arched entries that led from her foyer to her living room and onto her dining room. What did he think of her home?

"Would you like some tea or cocoa?"

"No, thank you. I should get going." Noah inclined his head toward the fluffy black-and-white-patterned armchair and its matching ottoman. Both stood beside the second walnut wood bookcase in her foyer. "Is that your Retirement Chair?"

Gwen's eyes caressed her relatively new purchase. "Yes, it is. I haven't used it much yet."

"I hope that there are many years before you're able to use it regularly. After all we're putting ourselves through, the results of our abstinence should be long lasting. " Noah's expression sobered as he turned to her. His gaze was intense as though he was trying to read her mind – or their future.

He stepped closer, surrounding her again with his warmth and scent. Noah cupped her cheek with his left hand, then lowered his lips to hers. His taste was so sweet. His touch was spellbinding. Noah drew her more tightly against him. He nibbled her lips before caressing them with his tongue. Gwen's mouth opened, but he declined her invitation.

Noah pressed his cheek against hers. His evening stubble was rough against her skin. Gwen felt his breaths against her neck. She drilled her fingertips into the tight muscles along his shoulder blades. Slowly, Noah stepped back, releasing Gwen from his hold but not his spell.

"Sweet dreams." He turned and walked out her front door.

Gwen locked the door behind him with reluctance. Yes, tonight's dreams would be much sweeter than the nightmares that had kept her awake last night. But could she be satisfied with only dreams?

CHAPTER 11

"You're going to be great." Cynthia's smile was determinedly confident. It was as though she was trying to will that self-assurance to Gwen.

Gwen returned Cynthia's strong hug, then stepped back. She was waiting with Cynthia, Kenneth and Noah backstage in the Metropolitan Community Civic Center's auditorium. In her peripheral vision, she saw Dexter in the stage's opposite wing, chatting, laughing, and preening among his entourage.

It was the second week of May, three weeks and five days before the June fifth primary election. Dexter was ahead in the polls, but his lead was thin and within the margin of error. So was Gwen's optimism.

She was minutes from the dreaded second debate with Dexter. It was one month after the first debate, which had been a disaster. This was the last chance voters would have to compare her proposed policies with Dexter's political record head on. In other words, a lot was riding on her performance tonight. She'd need more than a hug.

"They won't need two hours." Kenneth crossed his arms over his broad chest. "It'll take five minutes to look at Jackson's record and realize he hasn't done anything."

Gwen turned to Noah. "Do you have any last-minute suggestions?"

It had been a month since the night Noah had taken her into his arms, kissed her and wished her sweet dreams. He'd made sure they'd had a chaperone ever since. Tonight, it was his administrative assistant, Sandy Weaks. But she could really use a hug from him. A pat on the shoulder. A handshake. Anything to feel his skin on hers.

"Just be yourself." Noah's voice was low and urgent. "And stay-"

"On message. I know." Gwen glanced at Sandy. The slender, twenty-something-year-old kept glancing between the growing audience in the theater, the notes on her writing tablet and her watch. Had Sandy yet realized that she and Noah were using the assistant as a shield? If so, she hadn't let on.

"Voters are responding to you." Kenneth sounded reassuring.

Cynthia tucked her hand into the crook of Kenneth's arm. "After this debate, you'll take the lead."

"By a significant margin." Kenneth checked his wristwatch. "We'd better get to our seats. You've got this."

"Don't let Dexter distract you." Noah didn't touch her, but his eyes spoke volumes. They expressed his confidence in her, his admiration and his desires. Gwen's breath caught in her throat. He made her feel as though she could do anything. And as though she was everything to him.

Kenneth escorted Cynthia away. Noah turned to follow them.

"Good luck, Ms. Taylor!" Sarah called over her shoulder as she hurried after their group.

Gwen looked to the opposite stage wing. Dexter's team also was leaving. The senator caught her eye and gave her a mocking salute. Gwen gritted her teeth in a parody of a smile. She really disliked that man.

She squared her shoulders, took a cleansing breath and waited for the introductions that would signal the start of their two-hour debate.

Stay on message. Stay on message.

Fifty minutes later, the audience applauded another one of Dexter's false attacks against her. Dexter smiled as he waited for a break in his tribute. Gwen gripped her composure with both fists. She was afraid to even glance at Noah. Or Cynthia. Or Kenneth. Or Sandy. She was letting them all down. But she had help in the personage of the incumbent senator. He was twisting every word she spoke and misquoting every interview she'd given. And the audience believed him.

Stay on message. Stay on message.

The moderator raised his voice ineffectively over the audience's whistles and catcalls. "Please. Please. As I've explained before, we have limited time. Please hold your applause for the *end* of the program."

Dexter gestured toward Gwen. "My opponent has spent the better part of her campaign attacking our brave men and women in law enforcement."

"Senator." Gwen held up a hand to cut him off. "If my interest in preventing the unjustified killings of innocent people by police officers makes me anti-law enforcement, what does your refusal to even acknowledge these murders make *you*?"

Dexter glanced down at the notes on his podium. "Each year that I've been in office, I've championed increased funding for our brave men in blue – and the women. While my opponent tears down law enforcement."

Stay on message. Stay on message.

"Senator, please answer my question."

"Our community needs a senator who has government experience." Dexter stood behind his podium and gestured toward Gwen. "My opponent doesn't have experience in government."

Screw *the message.*

"Sitting in a government office while ignoring the people who put you there only gives you experience with sitting on a taxpayer-funded chair." Gwen watched the senator's face flush. "We need to usher *in* public servants and escort *out* politicians like *you.*"

Silence slammed into the theater.

Dexter's face darkened. He marched to Gwen and jabbed a finger inches from her face, ignoring the gasps and boos from the previously supportive audience. "I. *Am.* Serving the public."

"Senator." The moderator's voice quivered with nerves. "Please return to your podium."

Dexter ignored the request.

"How are you serving your constituents?" Gwen met the fury in the senator's gaze with a challenge of her own.

"Senator Jackson, I'd like for you to return to your podium, please." The moderator repeated his timid request. The audience continued to boo and hiss at Dexter's actions.

Gwen continued, defying the warning in Dexter's eyes. "You haven't held a town hall meeting in more than five years. I've volunteered at local pantries and homeless shelters. I've worked with community rights groups. Unlike you, I've listened to my neighbors. I know what keeps my community up at night, preying on their fears. I share many of the same concerns."

Dexter's face twisted with anger. "I don't need a town hall to tell me what people are thinking."

"Senator-"

Gwen interrupted the moderator. "Then how do you communicate with your constituents? Telepathically?"

"Dexter! Get back to your podium!"

Startled, Gwen's head turned toward the audience. The command had come from Noah. She located him sitting next to Cynthia in the front row. Cynthia's hand was on Noah's right shoulder as though she was pressing him back onto his seat.

The barked words seemed to snap Dexter out of his fog. He smoothed his tie as he turned back to his podium. "Excuse me," he mumbled into his microphone. "My passion for my work representing law ... well, not just the police but every ... every member ... of our ... our community. I got ... I was caught up in it."

Gwen gave Dexter a skeptical look. Surely, he realized that no one in the room bought his excuse. A somber mood wrapped around the audience.

Questions from the moderator continued, but Dexter wasn't able to recover his composure after his debacle. Gwen did her best to capitalize on Dexter's loss of self-control. As he struggled and failed to regain his confidence, it became clear that Dexter didn't have any plans for the future of their community. Hope cautiously took root in Gwen's heart. Would she be able to take the lead?

***

"I told you, you'd nailed it." Noah cradled his cellular phone between his cheek and shoulder as he spoke with Gwen. It was a few minutes before eight o'clock Friday morning, but his candidate was already hard at work at the library. Had she slept at all? "*The Daily*'s editorial board also stated in its column that, after last night's debate, it was changing its support to you."

Noah had called Gwen after his first reading of *The Daily*'s front page article reporting on her victory over the incumbent senator in last night's debate. He couldn't stop grinning as he re-read certain sentences in the news story.

"Taylor was confident and prepared during the debate ..."

"The party's challenger was knowledgeable about issues concerning the district, making the incumbent appear uninformed and disinterested..."

"I read it." Gwen sounded breathless with amazement. "The editors also encouraged the party to support me in the general election. Doesn't that suggest that they think I'll win the primary?"

"Yes, it does and I'm sure Dexter is furious." A fission of concern planted its roots in the back of Noah's mind. He laid the paper on his desk and fought to shrug off the feeling. "*The Daily*'s coverage, and the positive comments on television and radio news stations are strong boosts to our campaign. We need to capitalize on it. Yao said the online donations were pouring in overnight," Noah added, referring to his fund-raising director, Yao Fang.

"That's a relief. If we make it to the general, we'll need the additional funds." The rustling from Gwen's end of the call gave Noah the impression that she'd also lowered her newspaper.

"Bring the same energy and confidence that you showed last night to our final events and we'll make it to the general." Noah was certain Dexter was planning something. His mind raced with potential scenarios Dexter could use to derail their momentum during these final campaign weeks. "We're in the home stretch, but–"

"I know. 'The campaign isn't over until the voting polls close.'" There was concern laced with humor in Gwen's reply.

"We have to be on guard. Dexter's not used to losing. He's going to be angry that the spotlight has shifted away from him. That emotion will make him unpredictable."

Would Dexter attack Gwen's lack of experience? He'd done that and Gwen had turned that into a positive. Would he drop more snide innuendos about Noah's relationship with Gwen? Time and again he and Gwen had proven that their relationship was strictly professional.

"What do you think he'll do?" Gwen also seemed preoccupied with the concern.

"I don't know." Noah dragged a hand over his close-cropped hair. His elation over *The Daily*'s coverage of Gwen's successful debate was now a fond memory. "Let's be careful what we do and say over the next three-plus weeks. We don't want to give him ammunition."

Before ending their call, Noah confirmed their meeting that evening to review the agenda and Gwen's talking points for the state's medical association. For seconds that felt like minutes, he stared beyond the newspaper, trying to prepare a strategy for a political attack. Noah didn't know from where, what, when or how Dexter would strike. But he knew Dexter was planning something.

***

Noah choked on his coffee. On this first Sunday in June, *The Daily*'s morning headline stretched across its front page, "Taylor's Campaign Manager's Drinking Placed Sons in Danger."

What the ...

This was the primary surprise Dexter had concocted in a desperate, cowardly effort to sink Gwen's campaign. And it might just work. The state senator had waited more than three weeks and planted this story three days before the election.

Anger scalded Noah's skin. Disgust at himself, at Dexter, at the reporter – who hadn't bothered to contact him for a response – turned his stomach. With the paper clenched in his fists, Noah braced himself at his kitchen table before reading the story.

Ten minutes later, he was angrier than ever. The tactic was obvious. Unable to dig up dirt on Gwen, Dexter had turned the lens of his opposition research on Noah. Never before had he realized what a heavy liability he was to Gwen's campaign. That was his oversight – and now his crippling shame.

It could also very well destroy what was left of his relationship with his sons, especially James.

"Oh, Jamie." Noah punched Clark's phone number on his cellular phone as he jogged up to his bedroom to grab his sneakers.

"Clark-" The rest of Noah's words were cut off as his youngest son interrupted him.

"Dad, did you see today's *Daily*?"

"That's why I'm calling." Noah balanced his phone between his cheek and shoulder as he jerked on his sneakers. "I'm sorry about the article, Clark. Could you meet me at Jim's apartment? We need to talk."

"He won't talk. You know that." Clark sounded as anxious and frustrated as Noah felt.

"Then he can listen. Will you meet me?" Noah jogged back downstairs.

"Of course." They ended their call.

Noah shoved his phone into his front pants pocket. He grabbed his jacket, keys and wallet before jumping into his car and pointing it in the direction of James's apartment. Thirty minutes later, he pulled into James's apartment building's parking garage. He still had no idea what he'd say to his sons.

The elevator carried Noah up to James's apartment. Clark opened the door. His youngest son must have been watching for him. Noah entered the apartment and was confronted by James's unyielding back. His eldest son stood on the other side of the living room, staring out of the window. James must have seen him coming, too. And still kept his back to the door.

Noah shifted to face both of them. "Thank you for meeting with me. I'm sorry about the article in today's newspaper. I'm ashamed that *The Daily* dragged you into this with a reminder of one of the most painful times in our past. That night happened almost ten years ago. And you're both private citizens. You don't deserve this."

Clark shot a look toward James before meeting Noah's eyes. "It's not your fault, Dad."

"Then whose fault is it?" James spoke with his back to the room. He continued staring at his living room window. Noah was certain his eldest son's attention wasn't on the view.

"Mine. I've never denied that." Noah spoke carefully.

James turned. His eyes were angry. His voice was hard. "And it's all yours."

"That's right," Noah agreed.

"No one else's," James continued. "So what are you going to do about it? You can't ask for a retraction. It's all true. You can't give your side of the story. That'll only make you look worse. So what are you going to do?"

"The only thing I can do." Noah spread his arms, forcing himself to face the naked hatred in his son's eyes. "What I've been doing for years. What I'm doing right now. Ask for forgiveness."

Challenging the newspaper's reporting would further hurt Gwen's campaign. It would draw the public's attention away from the issues and toward his past. Even more importantly, James was right. There were minor inaccuracies in the reporting, but the essence of the story was true: his alcoholism had endangered his sons. The only thing that mattered now was earning his sons' forgiveness.

Clark shoved his hands into his front jeans pockets. "I forgave you years ago, Dad."

"Thank you." Noah was humbled and grateful. He turned to his oldest son. "James?"

"I won't forgive you." James's response came with a thick layer of frost.

Noah struggled to keep his voice steady. "I'm so very sorry that I wasn't there for you after your mother died. Tell me what I need to do to make amends and, son, I promise I'll try."

James fisted his hands at his sides. His voice was like sandpaper across Noah's soul. "Go back in time. Go back in time and change the past. *That's* what you can do. Undo all of the decisions you made that ruined my life, and I'll forgive you for all of them."

***

Late Sunday morning, Noah drove past Gwen's sunny yellow Toyota Corolla parked at the top of her street. She must be home. Had she read the newspaper?

Noah maneuvered into a parking space near Gwen's car. Though short, the walk up to her house helped clear his thoughts. The air was still as though bracing for an impending doom. Noah's latest encounter with James had shaken him. Badly. He rubbed his chest above his heart. Would he ever repair his relationship with his eldest son?

After his verbal thrashing from James, Noah had wanted to go home, but he hadn't. He couldn't. He needed to speak with Gwen first. He owed her at least that much.

How angry was she? Angry enough to fire him? Angry enough to want him out of her life – and for good this time? Maybe that was for the best. Considering their working relationship, would they ever be able to have a personal one? He'd hoped so, but he was certain he'd blown his chances. Again.

Noah jogged up the front stairs to Gwen's door. He took in the red, pink and yellow rosebushes blooming in the garden to the right of the steps. Even their beauty couldn't lighten the heaviness in his heart or ease the tension in his neck. Noah pressed Gwen's doorbell perhaps a bit longer than necessary.

He was prepared for her anger. Would it be directed toward him, the newspaper, Dexter – all of the above? Would she speak with him or would she rather not see him?

What must she think of me, a father more faithful to a bottle of Jack Daniels than to his sons?

Gwen opened her front door. Her cocoa eyes pinned him with an unfathomable look. "Perhaps I should have done a background check on you."

CHAPTER 12

Noah deserved that. "We need to talk. May I come in?"

Gwen's hesitation was almost imperceptible. She stepped back, allowing him in before locking her front door. Her shoulders lifted then settled as though she'd taken a deep, calming breath. Had it helped her?

"I'm sorry." Noah didn't know where else to start. He waited in the threshold between her foyer and living room.

Gwen faced him, but he was still unable to read her reaction. That didn't stop him from appreciating the attractive image she made in a flowing moss green dress that skimmed her slender curves. Had she recently returned from church?

"I just got off the phone with Cynthia." Gwen led him into her living room and gestured for him to sit on the sofa across the room from her red velvet armchair. The newspaper waited on the seat.

"What did she say?" Noah braced himself for Gwen's response. Cynthia was formidable and focused on this campaign.

"She told me to fire you."

Noah swallowed. Hard. "She's right." He still failed to read Gwen's reaction. She wasn't giving him anything to go on.

Gwen sat back, crossing her long, dancer's legs. A pair of orange ankle-high slipper socks protected her stockinged feet. "Is that what you want?"

"No." Noah stood from the sofa and took a few restless steps away from Gwen. "But it would be best for the campaign."

"You're putting the campaign above yourself?" Gwen seemed surprised. "I admire the new Noah more and more."

"We've already established that I've changed."

"More than I'd realized." Gwen glanced at the newspaper on her lap. "Why didn't you tell me you were a recovering alcoholic?"

Noah winced at Gwen's question. He turned to pace back across the room. "I was focused on you and the campaign."

"Oh, come on, Noah." Gwen crossed her arms and shook her head. "We've been working together since February. It's June. That's more than ample time to bring me up to speed on your past."

Gwen was right. Noah shrugged his shoulders, trying to ease the ache in those muscles. "It's not the kind of thing I'm used to talking about."

"Forgive me if I'm not empathetic." Gwen's tone was dry. "You did a background check on me, uncovering information about my parents' immigration status, my failed marriage and everything in between. Which of those things do you think was easy for me to discuss?"

"I can only apologize again." Perhaps Noah should have a T-shirt made with those familiar words. "I'm also offering to leave the campaign."

"With you gone, who'll manage the campaign?"

"The election's in two days. You, Cynthia and Kenneth can keep it going until then, and my team will still be available to you."

"If I'm still working with Barrow Consulting Group, I'm still working with you. Besides, I need you for more than the day-to-day management and preparation. I need you for moral support. I need *you*."

Noah stopped pacing. Did Gwen realize what she'd just said? Her words were an oasis of acceptance in the middle of one of the most humiliating days of his life. But was he reading too much into them?

He made himself meet Gwen's eyes. He saw confusion in their cocoa depths. And desire, but not for him; a desire for understanding. Yes, he was reading too much into her words.

"What do you want to do?" It was the question Noah should have started with.

"I want you to talk with me. Tell me what happened to put you in such a dark, destructive place?" Gwen's expression was patient as though she was willing to wait forever for him to give her the answers she sought.

Noah owed her that much and more. "I told you Joyce was murdered in 1999."

"I can tell you loved her very much." Gwen's voice was full of compassion. "I can only imagine how devastated you and your sons were by her murder."

"That's no excuse for the way I let her and my children down." Noah started pacing again as though he could put distance between himself and the inner demons that still plagued him. "I crawled into a bottle of Jack Daniels and it took me more than two and a half years to pull myself out. During that time, I put my kids through hell."

"But you did get sober."

"Thanks to James." Noah glanced over his shoulder at Gwen. "He wanted to go to college, but he didn't want to leave his little brother with a drunk so he called Child Protective Services."

"Oh, no." Gwen's expression of horror instantly transported Noah to that dark night more than ten years ago.

Noah scrubbed his face with his palms. "They threatened to take my children away unless I checked into a program and got myself clean. I've been sober since that night."

"Thank God."

Noah turned back to Gwen. "What do you want to do?"

Gwen rose. "I want to think over all of this. You know that I don't like making snap decisions, especially on such important matters."

Noah crossed to her. He stopped close enough to feel her warmth and smell her soft lavender scent. He wanted to touch her one more time in case he never saw her again. "I want to do what's best for you. And the campaign. I'll do whatever you want me to." *But I don't want to lose you.* The words were there, but he didn't speak them.

"I wish you had told me." Gwen searched his eyes. "I don't like surprises."

"I know. I wish I'd told you, too."

He wished he could go back in time as James had said to correct the myriad mistakes he'd made in his past. Those mistakes had cost him his son. They were about to cost him a client. Would they also cost him his heart?

***

"Thank you for coming so quickly." Gwen looked at Edwina, Cynthia and Kenneth as she served her guests a late morning snack of cheddar cheese, hard dough bread and ginger tea.

Her friends had joined her in her cozy dining room later Sunday morning to discuss how to address the media's negative news coverage of Noah.

Seated to Gwen's left, Cynthia sipped her tea before helping herself to the cheese and sliced bread. "We need to let Noah go. That's the best move for the campaign."

"He's become a liability." Beside Cynthia, Kenneth bit into his cheese and bread.

Gwen understood the power couple's point. She was a novice at the rules and strategies of political campaigns. Veteran candidates seemed to cut ties instantaneously with anyone who harmed their image - or were on the verge of harming their image - in any way. So why was Gwen waffling? Was her hesitation professional – or personal?

Edwina cradled her teacup. "It seems that we're all in agreement that we should cut ties. The only question left is how?"

Cynthia spread her hands. "We'll set up a press conference for this afternoon, and tell them that Noah's past doesn't reflect our campaign's reputation for responsibility and community."

Kenneth shrugged his broad shoulders under his casually elegant teal jersey. "That's standard. It's also true."

Gwen was uneasy with the discussion. Her gaze skimmed the framed pictures hanging on her pale yellow dining room wall. Each image – sunrises, meadows, mountains – included motivational quotes.

When people are determined, they can overcome anything. – Nelson Mandela

We may encounter many defeats, but we must not be defeated. – Maya Angelou

If you judge people, you have no time to love them. – Mother Teresa.

"There's just one problem." Gwen considered the untouched snack waiting on her powder blue dessert plate. The scent of the ginger tea was soothing. "Not all of us are in agreement that Noah has to go."

Cynthia's golden eyes widened. "You think we should keep him? Why?"

Edwina tilted her head toward Gwen. Her dark bob shone under the fluorescent recessed lighting. "You said that when Noah came to see you this morning, he offered to resign. Why didn't you accept his resignation?"

When they'd first settled around the table, Gwen had given her friends a brief summary of the conversation she'd had with Noah earlier that morning. Everyone had taken a moment to empathize with Noah's grief, but the discussion had quickly returned to the business at hand: What were they going to do about Noah?

She'd asked Cynthia, Kenneth and Edwina to join her because she respected their opinions and had expected they'd have diverse feedback. To her surprise, all three of them had echoed various versions of replacing the campaign manager.

Gwen glanced toward Edwina on her right. Her friend's crimson, long-sleeved blouse brightened the room. Gwen took her time answering, masking her uncertainty by slowly chewing a slice of cheese. The sharp taste popped on her tongue. "It didn't feel right."

Cynthia lowered her teacup. The silver threads woven through her braids perfectly matched her flowing silver A-line dress. "This is a political campaign. What do feelings have to do with it?"

Gwen had wondered the same thing until she'd remembered what Noah had said to her more than a month ago.

"I'm not running to be a politician. I'm running to be an advocate in office." Gwen lowered her teacup and looked to her friends, Kenneth and Cynthia on her left, Edwina to her right. "This campaign isn't about me. From the start, we've kept our focus on the people in our community and how I can address their needs."

"And Jackson has been trying to silence us," Kenneth said.

Cynthia rested her hand on Kenneth's forearm as if in agreement. "If we keep Noah, Dexter will win. He'll use Noah's association with us to continue to distract voters from our message."

Edwina gestured across the table toward the couple. "They have a good point, Gwen. You're ahead in the polls now, but it's a thin margin. After today, we'll still have two days before the election. That's plenty of time for the senator to drown out your message."

Gwen rubbed her forehead. "Releasing Noah is exactly what the senator wants. Noah wouldn't work for Dexter's campaign so he's trying to remove him from ours."

"That may be, but it doesn't change the fact that we now have a cloud hanging over us," Cynthia insisted. "We have to signal that our campaign is above reproach."

The chatter of the little voice in Gwen's gut was becoming more urgent. Cynthia, Kenneth and Edwina were right. Gwen knew that intellectually. This election was too important to risk even a whisper of scandal. Common sense and precedent set by other campaigns told Gwen that she had to replace Noah, preferably with someone who didn't have skeletons in his or her closet.

Still,… "What kind of message will we send if we condemn someone for his mistakes instead of acknowledging his redemption?"

***

The media was restless.

Gwen walked to the podium at the front of the community room in the Metropolitan Public Library late Sunday afternoon. It was the largest public meeting room in the library, but the crush of print journalists, broadcast reporters, cameramen, camerawomen and photographers made the space seem claustrophobic.

With Edwina's, Cynthia's and Kenneth's help, Gwen had pulled together the last-minute press conference with just enough time to get into the nightly news and morning papers. The meetings she'd had and the emotions she'd felt combined to make this one day feel like a week, but the tension tap dancing up and down her back made Gwen doubt she'd be able to sleep tonight.

At the podium, Gwen glanced at the notes she'd made before returning her attention to her audience. Her gaze settled on Edwina, Cynthia and Kenneth. The trio stood toward the back of the room. Gwen gave them credit for attempting encouraging expressions but she sensed their uncertainty. She also questioned whether she was doing the right thing. How would her decision affect their campaign?

She found Trevor Hollis, *The Daily* reporter, seated toward the front of the room. His article was the cause of their conflict. What did he expect from her announcement?

"Thank you for coming. I know this was very last minute." Gwen paused to acknowledge the silence that dropped dramatically into the room. "I want to address *The Daily's* article on my campaign manager, Noah Barrow."

Gwen took a deeper breath to control her emotions. "Mr. Barrow suffered a terrible tragedy. His wife, the mother of his then-two-young children, was callously gunned down by a domestic terrorist in 1999 while she attended her childhood church. I cannot imagine how devastated Mr. Barrow and his sons must have been and still are. Can you?"

She sensed the media's mood shifting from restless to pensive as though they were reacting to her words. "Imagine that your beloved spouse had traveled to another state to visit her family. And while she was in her family's church – a house of worship; a house of God – a mentally deranged domestic terrorist shot and killed her. How would you respond? What effect would that shock and grief have on you?"

Gwen paused again to let her question sink in. She hoped the media were still hearing her words. She continued, her voice slow and soft. "This tragedy happened almost thirteen years ago. There are some wounds that even time can't heal. But what time does allow is an opportunity for us to reveal our inner character. In response to his wife's murder, Mr. Barrow unfortunately reached rock bottom. He admitted that he became an alcoholic. But when faced with losing his children, Mr. Barrow turned his life around immediately for the sake of his two young sons."

Gwen straightened her shoulders and raised her chin. "Mr. Barrow's young sons are all grown up now. They've graduated with advance degrees and are gainfully employed. To quote the great Maya Angelou, 'We may encounter many defeats, but we must not be defeated.'" She continued. "I think we can all acknowledge that, due to extenuating circumstances, for a while, Mr. Barrow lost himself. He made mistakes. But what impresses me – what should impress all of us – is the way he corrected those mistakes. He found himself again. He did not let a terrorist's act destroy what remained of his family. Instead he let the love he has for his children help him find the strength to honor his deceased wife and her memory by raising two admirable people to help continue both of their legacies."

Gwen looked directly at the camera for the local government television station. "Let's be clear that Senator Jackson's vindictiveness is the only reason we're having this conversation. In his world, if Mr. Barrow wasn't going to be *his* campaign manager, then he'd make sure that Mr. Barrow wasn't going to be *anyone's* campaign manager. But the senator doesn't know Mr. Barrow very well and he certainly doesn't know me at all. After reading *The Daily* article, Mr. Barrow came to my home. He offered his resignation. I told him that I needed time to think about it. I don't make knee-jerk decisions. I've had time to consider the events of the past and Mr. Barrows's response to those events. I've decided that I will *not* accept Mr. Barrow's resignation. In fact, I'm proud to be associated with Mr. Barrow. There is no one else I would rather have managing my campaign. And now I'm happy to take your questions."

The media interrogation was fast and furious.

"Had Noah Barrow told you he was a recovering alcoholic?" This question came from one of the television reporters.

Gwen decided to keep her answer brief. "No." She pointed to a National Public Radio reporter.

"Were you disappointed that he'd withheld information about his past?"

"That's a complicated question." Gwen considered her answer. "Have you ever suffered a personal loss?"

The National Public Radio reporter nodded. "Yes, I have."

"You have my sympathies." Gwen paused. "Yes, I was disappointed at first. But like you, I understand that it's hard to discuss such a painful and personal tragedy. So I understand why he didn't immediately tell me. I also appreciate that he came to me once *The Daily* article ran."

Trevor Hollis raised his hand. Gwen was tempted to ignore him, but decided such a reaction was too petty. She signaled the reporter.

Trevor lowered his arm. "Are you going easy on your campaign manager because the two of you have a personal as well as a professional relationship?"

Gwen arched an eyebrow. "You seem rather obsessed with my nonexistent personal life, Mr. Hollis. May I ask why?"

Laughter rolled around the room, bringing a blush to Trevor's pale cheeks. "It's just that there's a rumor-"

Gwen feigned confusion. "The only rumor I'm aware of is the one started by Senator Jackson and which I've already denied. Is there yet *another* rumor?"

Trevor glanced around the room as though seeking backup. None was forthcoming. "I don't know ..."

Gwen started to step away from the podium, then turned back. She saw the fear dawning on Edwina's, Cynthia's and Kenneth's expressions before she shifted her attention to the media. "Noah Barrow is a good man and I admire him. He's smart, ambitious and funny. He believes in me and he's passionate about our community." Gwen held Trevor's eyes. "So for the record, yes, I'm attracted to my campaign manager and as of this moment, I'm going to stop fighting it. But my attraction doesn't have any bearing on my whether I'm prepared to serve my community. I'm prepared to serve. If elected, I'll commit myself to representing my neighbors' needs while in office just as I have been doing in my private life."

Gwen stepped away from the podium ignoring Trevor's look of satisfaction and the barrage of follow-up questions. She led Edwina, Cynthia and Kenneth from the meeting room, trying and failing to ignore their looks of shared concern. She didn't doubt that Dexter had watched her press conference.

Who had done more damage to her campaign, Dexter with his exposure of Noah's past or her by admitting to her feelings for Noah? It wouldn't take long to find out. The election was less than three days away.

CHAPTER 13

Noah collapsed onto his black leather sofa. He and Gwen spent months denying their mutual desire for the sake of the campaign. After all of that, Gwen had just told the entire state that they were attracted to each other. No wonder his business phone line had started ringing nonstop as soon as Gwen's press conference had ended. The media wanted his response. They could hold their breath.

Gwen hadn't fired him. Even better than that, she'd defended him. She'd put his feelings and experiences into words he hadn't been able to find in almost thirteen years. Noah started to rise to pace his living room, but his legs were still weak with surprise. For now, he was limited to either crying with relief or laughing with joy.

Noah was considering his choices when his personal cell phone rang. James's name appeared on his caller identification. "Jamie?"

"Dad?" James's voice was so thick with emotion it was almost unrecognizable.

Noah sprang from the sofa in a panic. "What's wrong?"

"I saw Gwen Taylor's press conference." A watery cough sneaked down the phone line. "She's right. It's not the mistakes that we make that matter. It's how we make amends for them. Dad, I'm so sorry."

For the second time that night, Noah fell back onto his sofa. His eyes burned with tears. Emotion clogged his throat. He tried to swallow past it. "I'm the one who's sorry, son."

"You were right. I wasn't angry with you. I was angry with myself." James's voice broke. "I tried to put my younger brother in foster care so that I could go to college."

"Jamie, you were trying to protect Clark." Noah's voice was firm. "Everyone understands that. None of this is your fault. It's all my fault. I should never have put you in that position. For that I'm so sorry."

James's laughter was steadier this time. "All right. We're both sorry and we both forgive each other."

Noah rubbed his eyes. His hand came away wet. "Thank you, son."

They spoke for a long time. Noah shed a few more tears before they ended their first nonaggressive conversation in more than a decade. Noah's heart finally felt whole. He owed that to Gwen.

***

"You gave me back my son. Thank you." Noah's words were the last thing Gwen had expected to hear when she opened her front door Sunday night.

"I'm glad, but how did I do that?" Gwen stepped back to let her campaign manager into her home. He brought with him the fragrances of the late spring evening – earth, grass and blossoms – as well as his personal scent. Gwen's heart fluttered.

"What you said during your presser connected with my oldest son, James." Noah's words came from behind her as she led him into her living room. He followed her onto her sofa. "He called me. We talked for more than an hour. It was the first time in thirteen years that we had an actual conversation."

His words took Gwen's breath away. "Oh, Noah. I'm so happy for both of you."

"So am I." Noah's smile was self-deprecating. "Your message resonated with me, too. I was so focused on the past that I never viewed my actions as redemptive. Because of you, I'm starting to forgive myself."

Gwen squeezed Noah's hand as it lay between them on the sofa. "You need to forgive yourself. In the end, you didn't let Joyce down. You took care of her kids and they turned out very well."

"I want you to meet my sons." Noah turned his hand around to hold Gwen's.

Gwen felt a familiar, exciting energy rush up her forearm. "I'd like that."

"You took a risk with your presser. Conventional wisdom is to cut ties with the source of a scandal."

Did Noah realize that he was stroking his thumb over Gwen's palm? She did.

"I know but I'd rather the campaign failed with my telling the truth than have it succeed based on lies."

Noah held her gaze. "You also publicly claimed that you're attracted to me."

Gwen's gaze dropped to Noah's full, firm lips. "That's the truth, too." Her words were a whisper.

Noah's throat muscles flexed. "What are we going to do about it?" he whispered back.

Gwen turned toward Noah and let him take her into his arms. She felt right there. Safe. And strong. His warmth enfolded her. Her eyes drifted closed as she breathed in his scent. Over the decades, she'd never forgotten it. It had lain dormant in a corner of her mind wrapped in memories of this man for so long.

Noah's arm slipped from around her waist. His hand cupped her chin and tilted her face up to see him. His gaze locked with hers. The passion heating his midnight eyes once again reached her, stirring feelings she'd been denying for the past three months. She wouldn't deny them any longer.

Gwen twined her arms around his neck and drew his head down to hers. Noah's mouth covered hers. His lips were firm, warm, intoxicating. Gwen sighed against them. She'd never expected to feel this way again. Not after her disillusioning divorce, followed by even more disastrous dates. Those experiences had made her feel so unwanted, unappealing, unattractive. Now, in Noah's arms, she felt empowered, desirable, confident.

Gwen pressed her tongue against the seam of Noah's lips. He opened for her. Gwen stroked her tongue against Noah. He groaned into her mouth. Gwen swallowed the sound. Noah's hands molded her torso in one long, slow caress. His right hand palmed her breast. Gwen felt his heat through her cream knit sweater. Her nipples tightened. Her core moistened.

"Noah." She whispered his name into his mouth. "Not here."

"Anywhere," he whispered back. But he freed her from his embrace.

Gwen took Noah's hand, rising with him from the sofa. She led him up the stairs and to her bedroom at the end of the hallway. Her knees were shaking. With each step closer to her room, her heart beat harder and louder. An electric charge coursed through her body.

She stopped at the foot of her bed and turned to Noah.

He kissed her softly and sweetly. "I'm clean."

"Squeaky," Gwen responded. She didn't even remember the last time she'd had sex, which told her how forgettable the experience had been. She already knew that tonight would be so very different.

Gwen was breathless as they helped each other take their clothes off. She was hot and restless by the time she and Noah landed in the middle of her bed. But Noah's movements slowed, signaling that he was going to take his time.

His kisses grew hotter and deeper, intensifying her desires and drawing them closer to the surface. His hands explored every inch of her and her body reacted to his silent commands. His fingers trailed over her hips and she turned toward him. His palms kneaded her breasts and she arched into him.

His lips exploited her pleasure points. He kissed her thighs, nipped her waist and suckled her breasts.

Gwen thought she would lose her mind. She looked up at Noah as he balanced above her. His features were tight with a desire that seemed to match her own. Gwen's body undulated beneath him, simulating what she wanted. Her legs parted, inviting him to join with her. Still, he denied her.

"Noah," Gwen whispered. "Please."

"Soon," he breathed against her ear.

Gwen groaned. It was time to take charge. She rose up and into him, rolling Noah onto his back beside her on the bed. Then she straddled him.

Noah's body tightened in reaction to the desire heating Gwen's cocoa eyes. He had to remind himself to breathe as he watched her, naked and straddling him on her bed.

"Do you want something?" He tried to tease, but his voice was gruff with arousal.

She smiled as she slid down his body. "You."

Noah moaned as Gwen explored his body with her lips and her hands, similar to the way he'd reacquainted himself with her body. Her fingers tangled in the hairs on his chest, then drew down his torso, leaving a trail of heat to his navel. Her lips and tongue followed the trail. Noah's breathing quickened. His muscles quaked. His body throbbed.

And then Gwen took him into her mouth. Noah's hips sprang from the mattress.

"Gwen." He felt her smile around him. It. Drove. Him. Wild. Noah's fists gripped her bedsheet and pressed into the mattress. His mind went blank. His reality shrank to her mouth, her tongue and her hands.

Gwen released him, allowing Noah to exhale. She shifted up to kiss him. Noah caught her hips and positioned her over him. He pressed his hips against her and surged into her core. She was hot, wet and tight. A wave of pure, carnal pleasure washed over him. Noah stilled as he and Gwen adjusted to each. In the stillness of the room, he could hear their breaths, deep and fast. And then Gwen moved on him. She arched her back and rode his length. His body strained toward completion even as he wanted this moment and these feelings to last.

This is where he was meant to be. This time. This place. With this woman. He'd loved Joyce. A part of him always would. But every step and stumble he'd made on his journey had led him here.

"Noah!" Gwen's body stiffened as she called his name.

Noah rose into her once, twice and again before his body also stiffened, and they collapsed together.

EPILOGUE

"Congratulations." Soon-to-be former State Senator Dexter Jackson made the praise sound like an expletive.

Gwen stood backstage in the hotel ballroom, speaking with her political rival on Noah's cell phone. It was just after eleven o'clock Tuesday night. Moments ago, Dexter had called to concede the election. With just over seventy percent of the precincts reporting, Gwen held tenaciously to a solid, double-digit lead in votes over Dexter. She still couldn't believe it.

Gwen looked at the small but mighty group of friends and family who beamed back at her. Cynthia, Kenneth and Edwina took center stage. Drew and Maggie had surprised Gwen by coming home. Her children had insisted they'd thought she'd realized they'd be with her for the election. James and Clark stood on their father's right. Gwen was on Noah's left.

"Thank you, Senator." Gwen felt as though she was glowing from the inside out. "Can I count on your support in the general election?"

Dexter's pause wasn't encouraging. "I'll think about it." He ended their call with those less-than-encouraging words.

Gwen returned Noah's cell phone with her thanks. "Senator Jackson isn't quite ready to endorse our campaign."

Cynthia threw back her head in genuine amusement. "Give him time to lick his wounds."

"Congratulations, Mom! You did it!" Maggie started the round of group hugs.

"I haven't done anything yet, but I will. Noah and I have plans." Gwen hugged Drew as tightly as she could.

Edwina, Cynthia and Kenneth pulled her into a victory squeeze. Noah's son James gave Gwen an awkward hug, but Clark made up for it with exuberance.

Gwen turned to Noah, took his face in her hands and planted a kiss on his lips. "Thank you."

Noah's eyes twinkled down at her. "Thank *you.*"

Gwen took to the stage to acknowledge her campaign's success and thank the battalion of volunteers who'd helped to make it possible. She studied the crowded room of mostly familiar faces while she waited for a lull in the cheers and applause.

"We started this campaign to send a simple message." Gwen was almost overcome with emotion. "That it's way past time for our representatives to acknowledge that they are our *public servants.* It's way past time for them to address the grave concerns we have about gun violence, about police brutality, and about a growing litany of other critical issues threatening our communities. We're going to continue to send this simple message during the general election until – win, lose or draw – our voices are heard and these problems are solved."

The audience went wild. Gwen took another moment for her heart to settle. "I'm so grateful to you for all of your hard work, your support and your encouragement. Thank you so very much. We wouldn't have made it to this leg of our journey without you or our brilliant campaign manager, Noah Barrow."

Gwen turned toward Noah who stood backstage and extended her hand. When he joined her, Gwen kissed him again. The crowd's cheers grew even louder and more enthusiastic.

Gwen smiled into Noah's eyes. "My first constituent poll, and it seems the voters approve."

Noah's gaze caressed her face. "So do I."

***

Decades: A Journey of African American Romance; *12 books, 12 authors, 1 journey. Start the journey from the beginning with the first book,* A Delicate Affair *by Lindsay Evans. For a preview, read the excerpt below.*

A Delicate Affair by Lindsay Evans
Chapter 1

Golden knew he was in trouble when she walked in.

Brown skin, thick hair, a lioness of a woman striding with a pride of other beauties wearing expensive dresses. They were obviously rich. Young. At least, younger than the crowd that usually ended up at Rosie's juke joint. Younger than Golden's twenty-six. More than half the men in the crowded, smoky dance bar turned to watch the three of them, but he only saw her.

Clive, a guy Golden trusted and who was the reason he had the luck of playing at Rosie's in the first place, jerked his head up from the piano and tilted his head at Golden. The sign for, "What's going on?"

Damn. Ten years, on-and-off, of being friends with Golden apparently gave Clive a clue when Golden's attention veered away from where it should have been.

Golden tipped his head toward the door. Clive, not missing a single key on the piano he played like a madman, looked over at the girls. No way would his friend know which one had made Golden just about swallow his tongue.

"No chance." His friend merely mouthed the words, rolled his eyes, and gave his full attention to the ragtime he pounded out of the piano, placed sideways so Clive could see the audience and rile them up when he stood, shaking out one long leg and then the other, dancing while he played. The music-hungry Saturday night crowd ate it up.

In front of the stage, the sunken dance floor was packed body-to-body. People danced and gyrated and generally had a good-old time while the music played. Marley, the only woman in their band of four, belted out songs about heartbreak and lust while Winston, quiet and quietly intense, tormented the crowd with a rhythm from his pair of tall African drums.

Even though the place was crammed packed to the rafters, Big Ed, the galoot by the front door, hustled over to take care of the giggling girls. He waved them toward a table near the front of the stage and off the side from the dancers. Damn near within touching distance, if Golden got bold enough. He plucked at the strings of his banjo, improvising around Clive's loud and lively rag.

Golden's fingers were sore from playing all night, but he was having too much fun to care. The crowd was jumping and that girl was hot as the fire in his mama's kitchen.

Watching her, he didn't so much as twitch the wrong way. He couldn't mess up the music. Only he—and Clive—knew he was sweating like a hog at the butcher with that fine girl breezing between tables to sit at the big one up front.

Golden knew Rosie, the owner of the juke joint and a notoriously ornery woman, had been saving the main table for her man. But as soon as the girls gestured toward the table with their perfumed and pampered fingers, Rosie gave it up easier than a whore on Saturday night. Those rich girls meant money in her pocket.

Golden had only been in Washington, D.C. for about seven months, but he had already seen what money and power could buy. The only difference up here was that the money and influence was thrown around by Negroes, and people jumped up mighty quick to do whatever these rich Negroes wanted.

The band's latest song wound down to almost nothing and, suddenly, Golden felt everything he'd been too lost in the music to notice before. The sweat running down his face. The rough chafing of the new suit at his wrists every time he moved his hands along the banjo. The hunger that cramped his belly from not eating since his morning shift at Joe's, the restaurant where he worked most days.

Anyone not dancing clapped and jumped to their feet while the rich girls spread themselves around the table, chattering with each other and looking around like they were at a zoo or something. With their bright clothes and brighter laughter, they were like the gems scattered in his mama's jewelry box.

One girl wore red, another green. But the one he couldn't keep his eyes off wore white. Bits of the dress sparkled, and she seemed like a diamond among the others. Expensive and untouchable, cool despite her loud and frequent laughter.

From the way they leaned toward Big Ed and stopped him from walking off, Golden could tell they were demanding drinks. But Big Ed shook his head and gestured back toward the kitchen, where the waitresses were tending to the other customers' drink and food orders. After another emphatic shake of Big Ed's massive noggin, the girls seemed to simmer down. Ed shuffled away as fast as his big body could carry him.

"More! More! More!" The crowd chanted and stomped their feet the way they did every night when the music stopped even for a minute.

The girls settled down and, with a few ringing notes on the piano keys, Clive started up another number. Golden wiped his forehead with the already damp rag he carried in his pocket, stretched his fingers, then poured himself back into the music.

For the length of another set, he managed to forget about the diamond girl and her glittering friends. But at the end of the set, the band scattered. Clive went off to find his girl lurking at the back of the bar, watching for any other woman ready to grab her man. Winston ran to the john to sniff whatever foolishness he had up his nose. Marley, who dressed every day in suits and ties, dipped out the back alley door to grab a smoke. Golden followed.

Instead of standing outside Rosie's back door like the customers did, Golden walked a few yards away to the awning of Swiss Jewel Emporium. The Emporium had been closed nearly a month now. In this neighborhood, it was tough for a high-class place like that, specializing in expensive watches and gems, to survive. Too bad, since Golden had liked the owners, two guys from someplace in Europe. They didn't chase him off when he came in nearly every day to gawk at the cases filled with glittering rings and necklaces. Those pretty things reminded him of his mother and her love of all things shiny.

Golden settled under the Emporium's awning with his back to the rough brick wall and a cigarette in his hand. He stiffened at the sound of footsteps and only relaxed when Marley made herself comfortable just a couple of feet away. He didn't tell her to kick off. As social as she could be, Marley had her own reasons for keeping away from the crowd gathered at Rosie's back door.

Golden was fresh to the city and still trying to get the hang of this smoking thing. Damn near everybody, including Clive, who he'd known back in Opal, said that real city men smoked. Golden didn't see the sense in it, but he had to admit it gave him the excuse to step away from the crowd and sit in his own quiet for a while. He still wasn't used to the rush and noise of the city, of people everywhere and the near-constant clang and clatter of his too-close neighbors. Sometimes, it was just too much. Although he was pushed out of Opal at the threat of a noose for looking at a white girl—which was bull because he preferred his girls as black as his coffee—Golden missed home.

He still longed for those quiet Southern evenings, nights of glow bugs and cicadas and the full moon burning a clear path across a field of peach trees. Seven months and he still yearned for all those things like crazy. But he wasn't returning to Georgia. He had a plan, and it didn't include moving backward.

"I'm heading to the john." Marley tossed her cigarette butt into a nearby puddle. Just before they'd got to the club that night, the rain had come and gone in a flash and left the streets wet but the skies clear.

"All right," Golden said, rolling his still-unlit cig between two fingers. "See you inside."

After Marley took off, Golden tucked the cig into the corner of his mouth and leaned into the bumpy bricks at his back. He loosened his muscles one at a time and breathed out around the cigarette, long and deep.

These days, it seemed to take a lot of work for him to relax.

He'd only just closed his eyes when the sound of raindrops drew him back to the present and into the musty alley. He looked up. From under the protection of the awning, the rain was almost nice. If the idea of walking back to his place in the rain and mud didn't threaten to ruin his one good pair of suit pants, he'd like it more.

Still, it was hard to be mad when a piece of the South visited him in the city like this. Light raindrops falling from the sky, lit by the streetlamps, aglow and surreal.

"That's not how you smoke a cigarette, you know."

The alley wasn't dark, but it was long, just a narrow strip between the building that housed Rosie's and the Emporium on one side and a combination liquor/department store on the other.

A woman walked toward Golden. It seemed like she materialized out of the air. She wore white and floated through the sprinkles of rain with an unlit smoke of her own held between long fingers. The diamond girl.

Golden almost swallowed his cigarette. It was only when he was fumbling to keep it from going down his throat that he heard a flurry of giggling conversation near Rosie's. What the hell? Two other girls stood between him and Rosie's door. They didn't look like they belonged anywhere near an alley. They watched him and Diamond Girl.

She came closer.

"Light me up?" Diamond Girl held the cig under her chin, protecting it from the raindrops sprinkling over her hair and pretty white dress.

The chain from a watch glinted gold against the dress and disappeared into a small pocket at her waist. The sight of her away from the noise and crowd punched him in the chest.

God *damn*, she was pretty.

Fighting breathlessness, Golden fumbled in his pocket for the silver match safe he hadn't yet pulled out for himself. He lit one of the matches with a flick of his fingernail and lifted the flame to the cig already at the girl's dark red lips. She sucked on the white stem of the cig. The tip flared red. In the combined glow from the lit cigarette and the street lamps, her skin looked dangerously soft.

Damn. Just…damn.

No way a woman should be that good looking and not be in a magazine, or a museum.

A smile blossomed on her face, like she knew what he was thinking. Blowing a plume of smoke to the side, she took the glowing cig from her mouth. "That's how you smoke, baby," she said.

He took the one out of his mouth, held it between two fingers, and looked down at it like it had done him some wrong. "It's not really my thing, anyway," he said. "Cigarettes make my mouth taste like ashes."

"Like ashes?" With the burning cig in one hand, elbow bent and balanced in the palm of her other hand, she quirked her moist lips. "What about my mouth, would it taste like ashes, too?"

Shock and a sudden blast of desire shot up Golden's spine. But while his brain was wrecked at the very thought of sipping from her rosy lips, his mouth opened up to save him. "Probably, and it's not a flavor I'm fond of," he said. "No matter where it's coming from."

The quality of the woman's smile changed, becoming less flirty and more flinty, like she'd taken his rejection to taste the cigarette from her mouth personally.

"You're not from around here, are you?" Just like before, she didn't wait for his response. She raised her voice. "Sounds like you just fell off a peach truck fresh from down South."

His fingers tightened around the unlit cigarette. Did this woman just…?

A rush of heat, part humiliation but mostly anger, scorched him from head to toe. Golden knew if they'd been in the bright sun, she would have been able to see every shade of furious red rushing under his pale yellow skin.

Giggles from her friends scurried at him like small spiders.

Golden shoved the match safe in his pocket hard enough to feel a seam break. "I come from somewhere it's considered uncouth and low class to be rude." He looked down at her from his height of just over six feet and realized, even in the midst of his anger, she was only a few inches shorter than he was, the perfect height for kissing.

Snarling at himself, he tucked the limp cigarette behind his ear and stalked toward the entrance of Rosie's, ignoring the pair of brightly dressed girls who gawked at him and giggled some more.

"Did you lose your catch, Leonie?" A woman's teasing voice rolled down the alley and followed him into the dance hall. One of Diamond Girl's friends.

Golden had always been a laid-back guy and never liked it when folks flew off the handle because somebody said something they didn't like. But, damn it if he didn't understand why they got so mad. Nothing made him more ornery than somebody treating him like an idiot just because he was from down South. Especially other Negroes.

Inside Rosie's, he waded through the press of hot bodies and the smell of booze to hop back on the stage.

"What's the word with the hot piece that followed you out to the alley?" Clive closed his fancy cigarette case and put a smoke between his lips. Like most people, he smoked inside the club.

He didn't need the same escape Golden did. "She looked hot for you, that's for sure."

"Nobody followed me anywhere. The girl was just getting some air with her friends."

"Didn't look like it to me."

"Seems like you better get your eyes checked then." He tried to make a joke of it with a slap to Clive's skinny shoulder.

Winston and Marley had already returned to the stage and were settling in. Marley tossed back her last swallow of liquor and slid the glass over the floor, out of everybody's way. At the front of the stage, she cleared her throat, getting ready.

"Let's make this money so I can go home with my girl," Winston said.

He wasn't the only one hoping to catch the slippery fish of success at the end of the line. Golden had his eye on bigger things, too. His dreams didn't end here in the nation's capital, where the colored help could play music all night long on stage but weren't allowed to sit at a table and enjoy the show with everyone else. Those whites-only places bothered him more than all the others. Here, Negroes like him were good enough to entertain but not human enough to deserve their own entertainment.

"Yeah," Clive said with a snicker. "And maybe Golden boy, here, can get that girl out there who's been eyeing him all night."

Golden snorted and grabbed his banjo. He played a few bars to warm up his fingers and then dove into the sweet shelter of his music. In front, the jewel girls sat at their fancy table, obviously eyeing him, but he managed to ignore them for the rest of the night.

In bed, much later that night, it was another story.

Diamond Girl found him in his dreams.

There, she was an ebony goddess with fire-red lips who hovered over him and teased him with her body. When she kissed him, she left the taste of ashes on his tongue. Golden woke up twisted in his sheets, his chest and belly heaving and damp with sweat from the lustful labor of his dreams. He burned.

His entire body was a hard and hungry ache not even the crude touch of his own hand could satisfy. A short while later, with the slick of his release drying on his hand and belly, he panted roughly at the ceiling.

If he never saw that girl again, it would be too soon.

Decades: A Journey of African American Romance
Continue the journey with these compelling, unforgettable stories:

January 2018: A Delicate Affair by Lindsay Evans (1900s), LindsayEvansWrites.com

February 2018: A Secret Desire by Kaia Danielle (1910s), https://about.me/kaiawrites'

March 2018: Love's Serenade by Sheryl Lister (1920s), Sheryl-Lister.com

April 2018: The Art of Love by Suzette Harrison (1930s), SDHBooks.com

May 2018: Love's Sweet Melody by Kianna Alexander (1940s), AuthorKiannaAlexander.com

June 2018: Pride and Passion by Carla Buchanan (1950s), Carla-Buchanan.com

July 2018: Promise Me a Dream by Wayne Jordan (1960s), WayneJordan.net

August 2018: Election Day by Keith Thomas Walker (1970s), KeithWalkerBooks.com

September 2018: Made to Hold You by Elle Wright (1980s), ElleWright.com

October 2018: Thug Love by Zuri Day (1990s), ZuriDay.com

November 2018: Inconsequential Circumstances by Denise Jeffries (2000s), DeniseJeffries.com

December 2018: Campaign for Her Heart by Patricia Sargeant (2010s), PatriciaSargeant.com

Thank you for reading *Campaign for Her Heart – Decades: A Journey of African American Romance, Book 12*. I hope you enjoyed the story. If you did, please help other readers find this book:

1. This book is lendable, so send it to a friend who you think might like it so she can discover me, too.
2. Help other people find this book by posting your review online (e.g., GoodReads, Amazon.com, BN.com, Kobo.com, etc.)
3. Subscribe to my enewsletter to find out about my upcoming releases.
4. Like my author Facebook page.
5. Follow me on Twitter.
6. Subscribe to my YouTube channel.